Tania del Rio!

Archie
Official Signed Edition

Diary
of a Girl
Next Door

Betty

Tania del Rio & Bill Galvan

DIARY
of a Girl Next Door:
Betty

Published by Archie Comic Publications, Inc.
325 Fayette Avenue, Mamaroneck, New York 10543-2318.
www.ArchieComics.com

FIRST PRINTING.

PRINTED IN USA.

Publisher's Cataloging-In-Publication Data
(Prepared by The Donohue Group, Inc.)

Del Rio, Tania.
    Diary of a girl next door, Betty / written by Tania Del Rio ; illustrated by
Bill Galvan ; inked by Bob Smith ; lettered by Jack Morelli.

        pages : illustrations ; cm. -- ([Riverdale diaries] ; [vol. 1])

    Summary: Freshman year is off to a rocky start with some major BFF
drama. Betty's longtime best friend Veronica is rich, ruthless and snobby--
the total opposite of Betty. And in high school, where social status means
everything, it seems like Betty and Veronica can't be besties anymore. Luckily,
Betty is armed with her trusty diary to document her ups and downs.

    Interest age level: 009-012.
    Issued also as an ebook.
    ISBN: 978-1-936975-37-2 (hard cover)

    1. Best friends--Comic books, strips, etc. 2. Teenage girls--Comic books,
strips, etc. 3. Diaries--Comic books, strips, etc. 4. Graphic novels. I. Galvan,
Bill. II. Smith, Bob (Bob A.), 1951- III. Morelli, Jack. IV. Title. V. Title: Betty

PN6727.D45 D53 2014
813/.6 [Fic]

Diary
of a Girl
Next Door
Betty

Written by **Tania del Rio**
Illustrated by **Bill Galvan**
Inked by **Bob Smith**
Lettered by **Jack Morelli**

Publisher/Co-CEO: Jon Goldwater
Co-CEO: Nancy Silberkleit
President: Mike Pellerito
Co-President/Editor-In-Chief: Victor Gorelick
Chief Creative Officer: Roberto Aguirre-Sacasa
Senior Vice President – Sales & Business Development: Jim Sokolowski
Senior Vice President – Publishing & Operations: Harold Buchholz
Senior Vice President – Publicity & Marketing: Alex Segura
Executive Director of Editorial: Paul Kaminski
Production Manager: Stephen Oswald
Project Coordinator & Book Design: Duncan McLachlan
Production: Suzannah Rowntree, Kari Silbergleit, Tito Peña, Carly Inglis
Editorial Assistant / Proofreader: Jamie Lee Rotante

THIS BOOK BELONGS TO:

_____

This person is super cool!

720 Days

Dear Diary,

It's time to panic.

This is the first day of my freshman year at Riverdale High School, which means there are approximately 720 days of school left until I graduate and have to go to college.

720 DAYS!!! That is like no time at all. And the worst thing about it is I have NO idea what I'm going to choose as my college major and time is running out to figure out what I want to be when I grow up.

This morning before I left for school, my mom seemed to notice that I looked a bit stressed.

She asked me if I was ok, and if I was nervous about starting high school today.

I admit I freaked out a bit.

NO! I'm nervous about what I'm going to do for the rest of my life! Today is just the beginning of the end of my youth!

Of course, my mom totally failed to see the seriousness of my situation.

She handed me my lunch and practically shoved me out the door saying, "Don't be so dramatic. Here's your lunch. There's a pudding cup inside!"

A pudding cup? Doesn't she realize I'm too old for those now?!

Jughead was at the bus stop when I got there. He also happens to be my next door neighbor. He's kind of weird, but we get along. (He gets in trouble a lot for sneaking food in class.)

I asked him if he realized that there were only about 720 days left of school before we graduate.

He also failed to see the seriousness of my situation.

When I got to school, I was able to forget about the 720 days thing for a bit because the place is so GINORMOUS!

High School (Ginormous)

Middle School (Basically a shack)

RIVERDALE HIGH SCHOOL

I was pretty much instantly lost.

Homeroom AB 3?! What does that even mean? Where am I ?!

After wandering around for a while, I decided I would just have to ask someone for directions. Yes, I know it's lame, but not as lame as showing up late to homeroom on your first day! (Plus, the earlier you are, the more likely you are to get a good seat!)

I saw some nice glossy looking girls up ahead to ask. They looked like juniors so they were sure to know their way around.

BIG MISTAKE. As soon as I started talking to them, they got all nasty!

I said, "Never mind," and tried to escape but then they seemed to feel bad. One of them said, "Come back! We're just kidding" and they apologized and said they'd show me where to go, so I decided to give them another chance.

I was relieved that they knew their way around because the school is seriously like a giant maze with so many twists and turns. Also, all the other kids seemed to step back and give us a lot of space. I guess these glossy girls have a lot of influence here! Maybe making friends with juniors isn't such a bad idea.

They led me to a door but it didn't have a room number on it.

"Here you are!" one of the Glossies said. "Room AB3."

"But where does it say that?" I asked, confused.

"It doesn't need to," one of the other girls said. "I mean, everyone knows this is room AB3. Go in and see for yourself."

So I did.

BIG MISTAKE.

I thought for sure I would be stuck there all day and be late to ALL my classes, but luckily the janitor came by before the late bell.

When he saw me he looked confused and said "What are you doing in here, young lady? This is a broom closet."

Yes, I had figured that much out by that point.

He was nice enough to show me the way to room AB3, though he was a bit too chatty.

As I entered my homeroom, I could hardly believe my luck. The seat next to Archie, the cutest boy in Riverdale--and who I've been crushing on since third grade--was still open!!!

I tried not to make it obvious how much I wanted to sit there, so I forced myself to walk towards it slooooowly, coolly, and confidently.

BIG MISTAKE.

I was so busy taking my time and playing it cool, I was totally intercepted by my best friend, Veronica Lodge, who apparently doesn't care how desperate she seems!

And, go figure, the only available seats left were in the last row where all the troublemakers like to sit. Like Reggie Mantle, for example.

He actually called me over and offered me the seat in front of his, which was still open.

BIG MISTAKE.

This is going to be a really long 720 days.

By the time lunch rolled around, I was starving. I could hardly wait to get to the cafeteria and EAT! (Now I'm starting to sound like Jughead.)

Veronica and I always used to sit together at lunchtime in middle school, but now she said she didn't want to eat lunch with me because she needs to "establish her place in the hierarchy" or whatever.

So now I had the intimidating job of figuring out where I was going to sit.

The Nerds' Table
Good: Interesting conversation
Bad: I'd become an instant outcast

The Goths' Table
Good: They're really deep
Bad: But soooo depressing

14

I can't BELIEVE Veronica betrayed me by going to sit with those Glossies! No, actually, wait--I can. BUT STILL!

I decided I would be bold and sit at an empty table all by myself. I would create my own clique of cool, like-minded people.

My Imagination

The Betties
Good: Smart, animal-loving, sporty, video game-playing, creative and fun!
Bad: NOTHING! Because it's my dream table

Of course, sitting alone at a lunch table waiting for a cool clique to form is a special sort of torture.

I thought I would be doomed to sit by myself for the entire lunch period, but then Jughead came along. He could care less about cliques or looking cool. (I'm not quite sure what that says about me and my table.)

I soon realized there was a big benefit to having Jughead at my table. I mean, HUGE. Archie was walking by, and Jughead waved him over and told him to sit with us. And before I knew it, Archie was sitting at MY table!!!

I could hardly move. I think I even forgot how to speak. I could NOT believe my luck! I began to think of all the implications. If Archie started sitting at my table, then he would become a part of MY clique! Next thing you know, we'd become even closer, like super good friends, and then, naturally, we'd start dating.

I CAN NOT BELIEVE HOW GOOD THIS SCHOOL YEAR IS TURNING OUT TO BE!!

Archie saw I had a pudding cup and was like, "Lucky!" so of course I let him have it. (I think Jughead was kind of annoyed with me over that...)

Of course, my good luck was not to last. Because guess who decided to stop by MY table? That's right, Veronica and the Glossies! I tried to tell them they weren't welcome there, but my mouth was full of peanut butter at THAT VERY MOMENT!

Veronica was all like, "Mind if we sit here?"

And all I could say was "MMmph! Mrrrmph!"

And then Archie jumped in and said, "Sure, there's plenty of room!" (GREAT.)

So basically, I had to endure Veronica and her new friends completely taking over the table (and Archie). But it's fine. I have roughly 720 days to figure out a way to win him back.

After lunch, I had chemistry. That's one of my favorite subjects and I'm seriously considering becoming some sort of scientist when I grow up. The teacher said we were going to have us split into pairs for the semester, but did she let us pick our partners? NO!! That would be too convenient.

And did I get paired with Archie? NO! Because that would have been too perfect.

The teacher paired me up with MOOSE! Ok, don't get me wrong. Moose is cool and all--but he belongs in a gym, not a science lab. And his girlfriend, Midge, has been shooting daggers at me ever since class started. It's not like it's MY fault I'm partnered with her guy! Geez!!

Anyway, I don't know why Midge is so upset. She got partnered with Dilton, who is one of the smartest kids I know. She's pretty much guaranteed to get an A in this class because of him! Meanwhile, I'm going to have to work extra hard to make up for Moose.

I could hardly wait for my next class--gym! If I don't become a scientist, I'm pretty sure I'll become some sort of athlete. Today we split into teams to play volleyball! And I got picked to be one of the team captains! Of course, I wanted to pick Moose to be on my team because what he lacks in science skills, he makes up for with a crazy spike.

But Veronica came over to me and begged me to pick her first. She said she can't stand being picked last, and if I was truly her friend, I would ask her to be on my team right away.

The problem is, Veronica hates volleyball and usually complains the whole time while we're playing.

I tried to offer a compromise. I would pick her second, after Moose.

But she said, "This is the thanks I get after bringing my friends to sit at YOUR lunch table to keep you company after we saw you sitting there all alone?" (Seriously?!)

I'm happy to say I held my ground, and I still went ahead and picked Moose first. Well, Ronnie was furious, especially when Reggie picked her to be on his team before I had a chance to recruit her. (She can't stand Reggie, but I think he has a crush on her.)

I tried to tell Ronnie I was sorry, but she said:

I think she's just being dramatic.

I think.

At least for the rest of the day it seemed that Veronica was holding to her word. She didn't speak to me in any of the rest of our classes. Not even in Spanish, when we were paired up to do speaking exercises.

AWKWARD.

By the end of the school day, I was BEAT. I can't believe I have to endure 719 more days of this.

When I finally got home, even though I already had piles of homework to do, all I wanted to do was faceplant my bed.

FACEPLANT!

After dinner I figured I should start on homework. (Who gives out homework on the first day of school?!! High school is so lame!) My dad wanted to watch a movie with me, but I was just too busy!

My dad poked into my room and said, "Hey, sport! Want to stream a movie on Webflix?"

I told him I couldn't, because I was TOTALLY swamped!!

He couldn't believe I had so much homework on my first day of school. I know, right?! SO unfair.

I could see Jughead across the way... but it didn't look like he was doing homework to me. It looked more like he was playing video games.

Maybe I should remind him that he only has 719 days left to improve his grades if he hopes to get into a decent college!

Slacker!

But then guess who I saw in Jughead's room, also not doing homework? ARCHIE!!!

(You know, I bet he already finished all his homework, which is why he was over there. He's responsible like that.)

I admit I watched them longer than I probably should have...

I should let Jughead know I like to play video games. Then maybe he'll invite me over too and I'll get to hang out with Archie more!

Also--guess who showed up at my door a bit later?

It was Veronica! And she acted like NOTHING happened earlier. She was holding a DVD and a bag of snacks and was all like, "Hey! I thought we could watch a movie! I brought popcorn!"

Of course, I was like, "I thought you were never speaking to me again!"

She just rolled her eyes and said, "Don't be so dramatic."

I tried telling her I had homework, but she just looked at me like I was speaking another language. And when I saw she had brought over the latest Yeti Thrill movie, I kind of forgot about homework.

Veronica and I love the Yeti Thrill movies. They're a series of horror films about a bunch of evil Yetis who live near various ski resorts. They like to kidnap and eat skiers. But they also like to break into elaborate dance sequences, which is mainly why we like to watch them.

Veronica has made me swear that I will NEVER tell ANYONE that she likes the Yeti Thrill movies. (To be honest, I don't really want anyone to know I like them either, so it works out OK.)

Of course, my dad wasn't too happy when he found us in the living room, hogging the TV. He said, "Too swamped to watch a movie, huh?"

I tried to make up for it by telling him it was Yeti Thrill and that he could watch it with us.

But he just shook his head and said "I never understood those movies..."

After the movie we went to my room to practice some Yeti Thrill dance choreography. I even found a couple old shaggy Halloween wigs that we put on to look more Yeti-like. We looked SO ridiculous!

I snuck a couple cell phone pics of Veronica when she wasn't looking. Who knows, maybe they'll come in handy some time! (Heh heh heh!)

I was having so much fun with Ronnie that I completely forgot about school. I got ready for bed and was halfway asleep when I suddenly remembered that I still had a bunch of homework to do.

26

So guess who was up until WAY past midnight doing homework?

Getting up the next morning was NOT FUN. It doesn't help that my mom is a total morning person and obnoxiously cheerful.

She's the kind of person who throws open the drapes and says things in a sing-song voice, like "Rise and shine, honeybee!"

What's worse, I think Jughead and Archie might have seen Ronnie and me dancing around my room last night! Jughead kept giving me funny looks at the bus stop! If Archie saw me in that stupid wig, I will DIE!!!

When I passed Veronica in homeroom, she completely gave me the cold shoulder.

Maybe she didn't see me? So I went up to her and said, "Hey, Ronnie!"

But she just turned away and said "I'm not speaking to you, remember?"

What the heck?! She's totally a different person outside of school. NOT COOL.

You know what else isn't cool? Finding out that all the homework I stayed up late to do isn't actually due until NEXT WEEK! No wonder no one was doing homework last night!

My teacher was really impressed, though. She said, "Wow, Betty! I love how seriously you're taking your studies. Keep it up, and you could be on track to graduate early!

EARLY?!

Oh, no. No way! I only have 719 days left as it is. The last thing I need is LESS time to figure out what I'm going to do with my life.

If only I were a dancing yeti. Life would be SO simple.

♡ Betty Cooper

Heroic Dog Training

Dear Diary,

I was watching TV the other day and saw this amazing show called "Dog Heroes" about dogs who jump out of helicopters and dig through avalanches and save lives and stuff.

I have to say, it was pretty inspiring.

I asked my mom if we could get a dog, and she looked annoyed and said, "Betty, we've been through this! Your father is allergic!"

My dad just shrugged and said, "Sorry, sport!"

I tried telling them that there ARE hypo-allergenic dogs out there, but they said those are too expensive. Now I think they're just making excuses! (And I'll have you know I'm allergic to dust, but my mom STILL makes me sweep the floors.)

I then told them that if I had a dog, I would train it to be really good and to do heroic things. I believe this far outweighs any allergic reactions my dad would (supposedly) have. Unfortunately, my parents didn't seem to agree.

When I brought it up over dinner, my mom looked even MORE annoyed and said, "If you want to be around dogs, find someone else who has them!"

"Fine! I will!" I told her.

I was mad, but my mom did give me an idea. I decided I would start my own heroic dog training service! In fact, I think this may just be the very thing I'm meant to do with my life. Think about it--if I start now, by the time I grow up, I'll be one of the top dog trainers in the country!

I might even have my own reality show! And besides, the world could definitely use more heroic dogs.

Of course, if I'm going to start a heroic dog training business, I need to come up with a suitable name and logo so people take me seriously.

So far, I've brainstormed the following ideas:

Hmm... I may need more time to think this through.

But whatever! The name can come later! What I need are CLIENTS. All it takes is one, really, because then I'll be legit.

And once I have a client, they'll be able to let all their friends know how heroic I made their dog and then business will be booming!

But where will I find my first dog to train?

When I saw Jughead at the bus stop the next morning, I asked him if Archie had a dog, but he said no.

Dangit! That would have been too perfect! Well, at least I can count on the fact that my business will impress Archie, even if he's not a client himself. He might even want to come work for me once I expand my business!

But the good news is I found out that Jughead has a dog named Hot Dog! "Would you like Hot Dog to be more... heroic?" I asked him. He just looked at me like I was crazy and said, "Huh?"

I explained my business plan to him. Then I asked him if he had any good ideas for names.

Yeah, barking mad!

HA. HA. Well he can be snarky all he wants. He still agreed to let me take Hot Dog after school and teach him a few tricks!

I decided I would start with teaching him to bark at danger, and then work up to rescuing people from burning buildings. I could hardly wait to get started!

Hot Dog

After school I picked up Hot Dog and took him to the park. I explained to him what the plan was.

People don't realize how smart dogs really are--you don't want to talk down to them! You have to treat them like the heroes they can be!

So I looked Jughead's dog in the eye and said "Ok, Hot Dog. I'm going to pretend to get into dangerous situations and I want you to bark whenever you think I'm about to get hurt!"

Dogs are also really good at picking up on feelings, so I tried my best to FEEL afraid in order to get a reaction.

After a few hours of working with him, I'm not so sure Hot Dog is hero material. He would have let me get hit by a car, fall into a pothole, leave my purse unattended, and eat gross street meat!

When I returned Hot Dog, I told Jughead that his dog lacked the ambition to become a hero and that he was probably depressed.

When I handed over the leash I told him, "I actually feel sorry for Hot Dog. He could have learned a lot if he put his mind to it.

But he clearly has bigger issues to work through first."

Jughead just gave me a weird look and said "Uh huh..."

He's CLEARLY in denial!

What I now realize is that I can't just grab any old dog and force it to be a hero. I need to recruit dogs who WANT to be heroes.

Once I had this epiphany I made an awesome flyer.

PUPS WITH PURPOSE!
Heroic Dog Training
by Betty Cooper

Is your dog RESTLESS? Is he tired of being like every other dog? Do you think he's capable of so much MORE? Do you want him to make a DIFFERENCE?

Then call ME! I'll teach YOU how to transform your dog into a SUPER PET!

You'll never have to be afraid again with your NEW dog at your side!

I spent all Saturday making the flyers. I added glitter and glued cotton balls on them and made each one unique. I want them to STAND OUT from all the other junky flyers you see everywhere.

I have to say, they turned out pretty nice. If I don't end up becoming a professional dog trainer, I may have to seriously consider becoming a graphic designer.

Next, I went around and put them up all over my neighborhood!

Now, all I had to do was wait for business to roll in!

I LITERALLY sat around all day Saturday just staring at my cell phone, waiting for it to ring.

I'm not proud.

Just when I began to give up hope that anyone would ever call, my phone rang! It was a lady all in a panic. She had seen my flyer and said her dog was definitely restless and could be a much better pet. Clearly he's a motivated dog who wants to do bigger and better things with his life. I told her she called the right place--I'd make her dog a super pet who saves people.

"Saves people?" she said. "I just want him to come when called!"

The next day I met with her to pick up her dog, Lucky. Man, he had a TON of energy. It was pretty obvious he couldn't wait to get started!

While Hot Dog was hard to get motivated, Lucky was a little TOO motivated. He dragged me straight to the park. At least he already has super-strength which will come in quite handy for being a hero dog.

At the park, I saw the perfect opportunity to train Lucky to be a hero. A cat was stuck in a tree and was in distress!

Now, obviously dogs can't climb trees, but I explained to Lucky that part of being a hero dog was figuring out solutions to complex problems. Well, you will not believe what happened. The minute Lucky noticed the cat, he got SUPER alert.

And then... HE CLIMBED THE TREE!!!

Unfortunately the cat didn't realize that Lucky was just trying to help, and it FLIPPED OUT! It literally jumped out of the tree and landed on all fours!

I tried telling Lucky that his job was done-- the cat was out of the tree, but he was too caught up in his heroics. The cat took off and Lucky started chasing after it!

I was FREAKING OUT. I chased Lucky all over the park. The cat was long gone, but he was still running around like crazy! I don't know what got into him! I guess it was an adrenaline rush. They say that performing acts of heroism can do that to you.

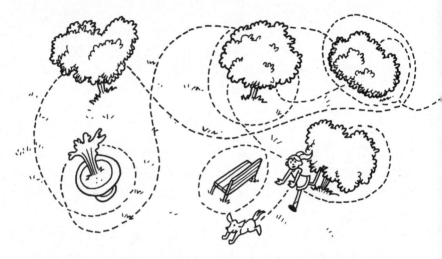

I began to think that maybe this dog wasn't so heroic after all, and just plain crazy. He began to do some very NON-HEROIC things.

Making kids cry

Terrorizing birds

Knocking over old people

Stealing food

It wasn't until he stopped to dig a hole in a plot of flowers that I was FINALLY able to catch up with him and grab his leash. What a nightmare!!!

But at least I still got paid when I dropped him off with his owner.

I was pretty exhausted from my day chasing Lucky around.

FACEPLANT!

I was super surprised to get a phone call later from Lucky's owner thanking me for everything. She said she barely recognized Lucky--he was sleeping peacefully all afternoon and was super calm when he woke up.

She told me Lucky had been transformed and that she was going to let all her friends know about my dog training service!

You will not believe it. The next thing I knew, I was getting bombarded with phone calls from dog owners begging me to transform their dogs. I even got in trouble in math class when my phone started ringing during a test.

The thing is, all these people who have been calling me seem to have really terrible problem dogs! That's hardly the hero material I'm looking for!

You will not believe some of the dogs people have sent to me.

But then again, the extra money IS nice. I guess it can't hurt to do what I can with these poor, dysfunctional animals.

Phew! Trying to train these terrors is SUCH hard work. I don't know if anything is sinking in, but I do know I'm so exhausted when I go to bed that I don't even hear my alarm in the morning!

I was pretty certain that the dog owners would catch on that I wasn't actually teaching their dogs anything, but I kept getting phone

calls telling me how great their dog was
acting, and I kept getting MORE business!

When Jughead saw me at the bus stop he
said, "So how's your Barking Mad business
going?"

I told him it was still going, but it was
EXHAUSTING.

He seemed to think this was funny and said,
"Well, at least you're getting lots of exercise."

That's when it hit me! The reason I'm having
success is not because I'm actually training
the dogs--it's because I'm EXERCISING them!

Half these dogs are probably ignored at home.
All they want is attention and a good run
around the park.

Well, once I figured that out, my job got WAY
easier.

But now I had a NEW problem. My business was getting so popular, I didn't have time for anything else!

For example, when my dad asked me if I wanted to shoot some hoops, I had to tell him, "I can't! I have to walk six dogs!"

And when Veronica asked me to go to the mall with her after school, I had to turn her down too, saying, "I can't! I have to walk eight dogs!"

And then, when my mom asked me what I wanted for dinner, I cried, "I can't eat! I have to walk TEN dogs!"

When I started getting too tired to do homework, that's when I knew I was in serious trouble.

FACEPLANT!

I considered hiring someone to help me out. But I guess no one else is as passionate about dogs as I am.

I asked Jughead, but he said "Sorry, I'm too lazy." Well, at least he's honest.

Veronica was just like, "You're kidding, right?" (Geez. Sor-ry!)

My mom rolled her eyes and said "I already have a job!"

And my dad said, "I'm allergic, remember?!"

Come to think of it, I'm not sure this is really what I want to do when I grow up anyway. I mean, the extra money is great, and it's cool to get to hang out with dogs, but it's definitely starting to get in the way of my life. As in, I DON'T HAVE ONE.

So I started letting all my clients know I wouldn't be able to walk their dogs anymore, except for a couple, whose dogs I actually like.

Of course, they were sad to hear it, but I did tell them that all they really had to do was walk their dog more often and they could save some money. You would think I was speaking gibberish!

One of my clients even got mad and said "You want me to walk him myself? I don't have time for that!"

Well maybe he shouldn't have gotten a dog in the FIRST PLACE!

I'm beginning to think what the world needs is a PEOPLE-training course, where they learn how to be better pet owners! Sheesh!!

Hmm... new business idea?

Just when I finally wrapped up my heroic training/dog walking business, you will not BELIEVE what happened!

We were eating dinner and my mom said that she and my dad were really proud of me, and impressed with how I've been handling my dog walking business.

I thought about telling them that I just ended it, but it didn't seem like a good time to do that.

Then my mom was like, "Your father and I have talked about it and decided we can look into getting a hypoallergenic dog!"

I think that news was supposed to make me happy, but all I could think was how much WORK having a new dog would be. And I would NEVER be able to escape that kind of responsibility!

Not only that, dogs can live for like, 15 years. And I only have 4 years left of high school-- which means I'll have a dog that I'm going to have to say GOODBYE to when I leave for college because dorms don't allow pets!

That's not fair to me OR the dog.

So I tried turning my parents down as gently as possible.

I told them that I'd had my fill of dogs for a while, but I'd LOVE to have a pony if they're still up for getting me a pet.

They didn't seem very amused.

Somehow, I don't think I'm going to get a pony.

♡ Betty Cooper

Peer Mediation

Dear Diary,

Riverdale High has a counselor called Mrs. King.
I guess someone found out her first name is
Joanne, and now everyone calls her "Jo King"
behind her back. (I don't think she likes that
very much.) As a result, she is one of the
most unpleasant school counselors I have ever
seen! (And she's not very funny at all, despite
her nickname.)

Every time I walk past her office, the door
is open, and she's sitting there waiting for a
student to come by. But no one ever does. In
fact, sometimes I feel kind of sorry for her.

I think Mr. Weatherbee feels sorry for her too
because one day he called an assembly just
to tell us that Mrs. King was available for
counseling. As if we didn't already know!

He was all like, "Blah, blah, blah, I encourage you all to visit her office--if you're being bullied or have troubles at home, she's here to listen and help. Etcetera, etcetera."

Then Reggie said, "You must be Jo-King!" and everyone laughed. Well, except for Mr. Weatherbee and Mrs. King.

Even after the assembly, I don't think many kids stopped by Mrs. King's office. I still felt kind of bad so I decided to invent a problem to see her about, just so she would feel useful at her job.

I made up a story about how my little brother can be such a jerk sometimes. And Mrs. King got really into it and was asking me all sorts of questions about how I handle conflicts when they come up, and was offering a bunch of suggestions.

I just hope she doesn't catch on to the fact that I don't actually have a little brother. I mean, I DO have two older siblings, but they don't live at home anymore, so I couldn't very well use them as my problem could I?

But, you know, I was starting to feel kind of guilty about lying to her. I guess I COULD have come up with a real problem instead of just making one up. But the truth is, I've always WANTED a little brother, even though he probably WOULD get on my nerves. Also, being the youngest child is pretty lame most of the time. You would THINK now that I'm the last kid living at home that I would get more attention and more presents, but this is NOT the case.

Anyway, I figured if there was any way to make having a little brother become a reality, I wouldn't have to feel as guilty about making things up.

I don't think my parents are on the same page.

Worse yet, every time I pass Mrs. King in the halls, she asks me how "Xander" is doing.

When I made up the story about my fictional

little brother, Xander was the only name I could think of off the top of my head, thanks to the main character of my favorite video game, "Reins of Fire".

Xander Kilburn, Dualicorn Mage

(Isn't he dreamy?) ♡

(At least I didn't call my fake brother Mi'talrythin, which is the name of my second-favorite video game character.)

Anyway, I can rest a bit easier knowing that because of the whole confidentiality thing, Mrs. King can't say anything about my make-believe brother in front of my friends. So my secret is SAFE!!!

I don't think my efforts to help Mrs. King out by visiting her office have done much good because Mr. Weatherbee called ANOTHER assembly to announce a new kind of counseling: peer mediation!

This time, he was all like, "Blah, blah, blah, it may be that some of you are not comfortable speaking to an adult, so this new program will give you a chance to support your fellow students while working through problems in a productive manner. Etcetera, etcetera."

He set up a ballot box and told us to vote for the classmates we felt would make the best peer mediators. Honestly, I'm not really even sure what that means, but I put Archie Andrews' name in the box because I'm pretty sure he'd be good at anything.

Of course, Veronica just assumed that everyone would be voting for her. (Go figure.)

She was saying things like, "Honestly, I don't know how I'll fit it into my schedule, but when the class chooses me to be their peer mediator, I'll just have to rise to the occasion!"

Then she looked at me with her no-nonsense gaze and said. "Betty, you DID vote for me, right?"

And I was like, "Um. Yeah."

Ugh, I'm turning into such a liar!!!

I don't see how Veronica could ever make a good peer mediator. She NEVER listens to anyone's problems and is only interested in talking about HERSELF!

The next day, Mr. Weatherbee announced the names of the two students who got the most votes and were picked to be peer mediators. Imagine my shock when he said:

And I thought I was going to pass out when he announced the second name.

I CAN'T believe it! Me and Archie! We're going to get to peer mediate together! It's like a dream come true! It's like being picked Prom King and Queen, except even BETTER because it's more intellectual and stuff!

Of course, I couldn't reveal how happy I actually was. I had to play it cool. Peer mediators have to be calm as can be, like 911 operators, because of all the problems we have to deal with.

Since I was aware that everyone was looking at me when my name was announced, I did my best to look like it was NBD.

But on the inside:

I seriously thought my knees would give out when Archie came up to me after the assembly and told me he was looking forward to being a peer mediator with me. How am I supposed to stay cool when being next to him makes me feel like a ball of jelly dorkishness?

Unfortunately, Veronica was furious. She was convinced there was a miscount in the ballots, and that the whole election was rigged. I don't think she would make a very good politician.

Hmm, then again, maybe she would.

After school, Archie and I had a meeting with Mrs. King about how to be good peer mediators. I tried to pay attention, but Archie smelled like peppermint gum and it was VERY distracting.

In fact, I can hardly remember what she said. Something about being impartial when dealing with conflicts... and about how important it is to be a good listener. Or something.

After the meeting, Archie walked me home. Okay, so maybe he was also on his way to hang out at Jughead's house, but I'll take it!

I just know we're going to become SUPER close because of our duties. They always say those kinds of responsibilities bring people together. We'll be dating in no time!

Unfortunately, I quickly realized that being a peer mediator is not nearly as glamorous as it sounds.

Here's why:

ONE: We have to give up our lunch breaks to do it!

TWO: People like Reggie keep abusing the system!

THREE: It's super awkward when you're friends with the people being mediated.

But sometimes it's really cool to be a peer mediator, like when you actually HELP someone solve a conflict.

And when Archie notices what a good job I'm doing.

ESPECIALLY when he notices what a good job I'm doing.

On the inside

In fact, not to toot my own horn or anything, but I actually think I've got a knack for this mediation stuff. I think there's a good chance that when I grow up I'll be some kind of mediator, but for adults. I bet I'll even have my own talk show where I help people with their problems.

I've even tried to mediate my parents' arguments.

Like, one day my mom was nagging my dad about rinsing the dishes in the sink before putting them in the dishwasher, because otherwise they get all crusty and then she has to wash them twice.

I could tell my dad was annoyed, but I cut in and said, "Dad, I think what I hear Mom saying is that she feels you don't value the extra work she does around the house, and that she cares about the environment."

But I don't think they realize I'm just trying to help.

Of course, just when I was starting to really enjoy peer mediation, Veronica had to go and RUIN it for me!

She came in one day and said she had a problem with a fellow student. Archie told her she'd have to bring the other student into the meeting, so that we could work it out with them both. And that's when she was like, "Oh, she's here all right. My problem is with BETTY!"

WHAT!! I tried telling her I couldn't very well mediate MYSELF with her, because that would go against the rule of being impartial!

But then Ronnie said Archie could mediate us, couldn't he? And he was forced to agree. What happened next was THE MOST AWKWARD PEER MEDIATION SESSION EVER!!!

When Archie asked her what the problem was, Veronica said "Betty has manipulated her way into getting close to a certain SOMEONE she likes and now she's completely abandoned our friendship!"

This was TERRIBLE! And it was a Catch-22! See, if Veronica revealed to Archie that HE was the one I liked, I would DIE from embarrassment. The End.

But then, if she DIDN'T reveal it, then Archie would think I liked someone ELSE and this would discourage him from ever asking me out!!!!

UGGGHHH! Sometimes I can NOT stand Veronica!

Because, if there's one thing Veronica can't stand, it's being called out, and she was FURIOUS. Before we knew it, we were fighting pretty bad.

Apparently we were being so loud, we attracted the attention of Mr. Weatherbee and Mrs. King all the way in the teachers' lounge.

They ended up bursting into the room and basically had to pull us apart.

So Veronica and I both got detention. I was MORTIFIED that Archie saw me lose control like that. Now he'll NEVER want to date me!

When we got to detention, Reggie was there and even held the door open for us saying, "Welcome, ladies, to my kingdom: Detention. Please, make yourself comfortable."

(Ms. Grundy yelled at him to sit down and be quiet after that.)

It was awkward having to sit next to Veronica after our fight. I tried to apologize, but she just ignored me and pretended I wasn't there. But she ignored Reggie too, so I didn't feel quite AS bad.

I was REALLY dreading the next time I would
have to see Archie again. I considered cutting
and dyeing my hair, and changing my name, and
pretending to be a foreign exchange student...
but I ruled that out because I'm not really
good at faking accents.

Of course, Jughead had to give me a hard time
when I saw him at the bus stop the next day.
He was all like, "I heard you and Ronnie had
an epic fight! How was your first detention
experience?"

How did he know about that?!

I was hoping he would say that Reggie told
him, but NO! Just my luck--Jughead said that
Archie told him ALL about it! I tried not to look

upset as he laughed at me and said, "Archie said he didn't know you had it in you."

But inside:

ARRRRGGGGHHHH!!!

As if I wasn't already humiliated enough, I got FIRED from being a peer mediator.

But why did they have to call both me AND Archie into the office to tell me? Oh, that's right—it's because they're trying to RUIN MY LIFE!

Mrs. King said that she was afraid I wasn't the right person for the job, so they were going to find someone else to step in.

But then the most AMAZING thing happened.

Archie stood up and said, "Actually, Mrs. King, if Betty isn't going to be a peer mediator anymore, then I don't want to be one either. I resign."

I think Mrs. King was upset. She looked like she swallowed a really sour lemon and told Mr.

Weatherbee to check the ballot again to see
which students the next two highest votes
were for.

Afterwards, I tried to thank Archie.
AWKWARDLY, of course.

I think things are going to be okay.

Archie even joked that they should have paid
us more, and that we should report them for
child labor. He said that he should sic me on
them, now that he's seen what I can do. I
guess I'm relieved we can joke about it, even
though I'm still mortified about losing my
temper.

A part of me is a little bummed it's over, but I'm also kind of relieved. I don't think I'm meant to be any kind of mediator after all.

The next day, Veronica bragged to me about how she was next in line to be a peer mediator.

She was like, "I can't WAIT to join Archie in helping our fellow students. We'll make such a good team!"

(I didn't have the heart to tell her that Archie quit.)

Anyway, it didn't take her long to find out. Word is, when she found out she was partnered with Dilton, she FLIPPED OUT!

Mr. Weatherbee ended up canceling the entire peer mediation program after that.

I can't help but feel a teensy bit responsible. But when Archie offered to walk me home a few days later, I couldn't believe my luck! I totally avoided any karmic backlash from that whole episode!

On the way out, we ran into Mrs. King, who asked me if things were going better for me now. I told her yes, and thank you.

But then she told me to say hello to Xander. And I was so frazzled I cried out:

I did the only thing I could think of to do. I ran away.

So Archie didn't end up walking me home after all.

Karma.

♡ Betty Cooper

BMX

I was online doing research for a history paper I had to write about the Dust Bowl, when I somehow ended up browsing videos on iTube. (You know how it happens...)

Anyway, I came across an awesome live-stream of the BlueZephyr Cola BMX games in California! I COULD NOT believe how crazy some of those BMXers were, going off ramps and doing sick flips. How do you even LEARN to do stuff like that?!

One of them was doing all these insane tricks and then when he was done he took off his helmet--only it wasn't a he. It was a GIRL! She is my new idol. Her name is Davey Starr and she is SO EPICALLY COOL!!!

I spent the next two hours visiting fan sites and learning EVERYTHING about her (for example, she was born in Iceland and she's been competing professionally since she was my age!). I AM OBSESSED!!

(I sort of forgot about my research paper. Oops.)

I decided if she was able to get her start as a BMXer at my age, so can I! I've always loved competitive sports--maybe this is what I can spend the rest of my life doing! Besides being a totally fun job, I'd also make tons of money from all my endorsements.

Only one problem: I don't have a BMX bike!

I went in the garage and pulled out my old beach cruiser. It's not great, but it will have to do for now.

Glitter Stickers from 4th grade

Rusty

Back Wheel Squeaks

Dented Fender

It's been a while since I've ridden it, so I had a quick ride around the block to get my "sea legs" back (har har).

They say you never forget how to ride a bike, but I'm a little embarrassed to say I was feeling pretty shaky! I'm just glad no one was able to see me.

Or so I thought.

Once I had ridden around enough that I felt back to being comfortable on two wheels, I decided to take it to the next level! I just needed a ramp to practice doing jumps with!

After digging around in the basement for a bit, I found the perfect thing! My dad's old bean bag toss game. He was out fishing with a buddy, so I couldn't ask him if I could use it, but I was sure he wouldn't mind!

I'll have to avoid riding over the hole, but that will just add to the dare-devilness of it all!!

Of course, that's easier said than done. On my first try, my wheel got stuck in the hole, and I flew off my bike!

But I was prepared--full safety gear is important with extreme sports! Earlier I had dug around in my closet and found my skateboarding helmet, knee and elbow pads, shin guards, wrist guards, shoulder pads, and gardening gloves!

Nothing can harm me now! WAH HAHAHA!

One thing I quickly learned is that all the padding in the world doesn't make up for the fact that a beach cruiser has NO SHOCKS. Landing off the ramp for the first time was like hitting a wall of bricks.

So I had to reinforce my landing with a couple of my mom's yoga mats. She was out running errands, so I couldn't ask her if I could use them, but I was sure she wouldn't mind.

But I never got a chance to see if my landing would have been improved...

It was clear I had the WRONG kind of bike for these kind of tricks. It's just TOO heavy and clunky, and can't absorb the shock of all the awesome tricks I want to do.

There's no way around it: I NEED a BMX bike!!!

But when I looked online to see how much
they cost, I could hardly believe my eyes. Sure,
I could MAYBE buy a cheapie one, but that
wouldn't be much better than my old beach
cruiser. If I'm going to be a professional BMXer,
I need to do this RIGHT! Which means getting
an expensive bike!

There's no way I could ever afford to buy a
BMX bike on my own, so I decided to ask my
parents if they would buy me one. My mom
told me it was too expensive and my dad asked
me what happened to all my money from my
dog walking business.

I told him I spent it all!

It's true. I DID have money at one time, but I
ended up using it to buy some limited edition

Yeti Thrill dolls imported from Japan. I guess it was a BIT impulsive to buy them all at once, but they do look pretty cool on my shelf.

I COULD wait until my birthday and see if my parents get me a BMX bike then, but that's still MONTHS away! If I want to make this a career, I need to start training NOW. I don't have time to waste!!!

Sometimes I wish my family was rich like Veronica's. She doesn't even realize how lucky she is!

She could have ANYTHING, but she spends all her spare money on clothes and jewelry. BORING!

Still, being her friend has its perks. I figured if I could convince Veronica to get a BMX bike, then I could use it too! And, knowing her, she'd probably get bored with it after a while, which would mean that I could use it pretty much whenever I wanted to!

It's the perfect plan, really!

Except for one problem. When I told her about it, she just snorted and said, "A BMX bike? Why would I want THAT? I don't even know what that is."

So I showed her some pictures and videos online of Davey Starr doing tricks. I thought for sure that this would convince her!

I was wrong.

Okay, now I know what it is. But still, why would I want THAT?

My plan was already in danger of failing! I needed to figure out a way to make Veronica WANT a BMX bike and fast!

So I decided to make a list of all the things Veronica likes to see if there was any crossover with BMX bikes.

Starting at the top of the list, I told her that getting a BMX bike would make her the most popular girl in school.

To which she responded, "Hahaha! Betty, you're so funny. I'm ALREADY the most popular girl in school! If anything, being seen on one of those silly little bikes will make me LESS popular. They look ridiculous!"

This was NOT going as planned.

I had to wait a few days before I brought it up again. But this time, I used the angle of it being the latest trend. I told her I read an article that there was a "BMX Boom" coming, and that soon, EVERYONE and their mother would have one. If she wanted to stay ahead of the curve, she should get one NOW, and then everyone would give her credit for starting the trend. If there's one thing Veronica likes, it's getting credit for things, even when it's not really her idea.

This technique actually seemed to be working at first! She was like, "Hmm... is that so?"

But then she said, "Wait a minute. You said you read this in an article? That means the BMX thing is ALREADY behind the times. The best trends aren't noticed and written about until they're practically over!"

Strike two.

Still, I would not be deterred! Next on my list: Shopping! If there's one thing Veronica loves, it's going to the mall. So when I suggested we take a trip there, she was ALL FOR IT!

Of course, first I had to endure us going into approximately 5 billion high-end clothing shops where I couldn't even afford a pair of pants, and I had to wait for her to try on approximately 5 billion things.

Finally, as we were heading out of the mall, we passed the sporting goods store. And just my luck, there was an awesome BMX in the window! So I tried dragging her in there to look at it with me. She was like, "SPORTING goods? Betty, do you SEE my manicure? I'll probably break a nail just by walking in!"

She put up a fight, but I was finally able to convince her to go in with me and look at the bike in person. She did not look impressed.

I told her it looked cute, and that the color totally matched her eyes. She looked like she was actually considering it, and asked if it came in hot pink! I thought for sure that I had her, until she spotted the GLOSSIES walking by outside.

She just told me that she had a reputation to uphold and she couldn't be seen in a place that sold tackle boxes and camouflage. I told her tackle boxes make great makeup organizers, but she didn't care. She dragged me out of there... and away from my beloved bike!

Strike three!!!

Next on my list was "Winning." Ronnie LOVES to win, so I used my supreme art and graphic design skills to create a flyer for a pretend BMX contest. I know Ronnie wouldn't be interested in dangerous stunts, so I tried to make it appeal to the things she likes.

It was pretty convincing if I say so myself.
In fact, I wish there WAS a contest like that,
because that would be pretty sweet, don't
you think?! Anyway, I figured I'd just wait for
Veronica to buy her bike, and then I'd tell her
the event was sadly canceled.

Ok, so maybe it's not very nice to fake her
out like this... but I'm getting DESPERATE!!!!

I printed out a few copies and left them where
I knew she would find them.

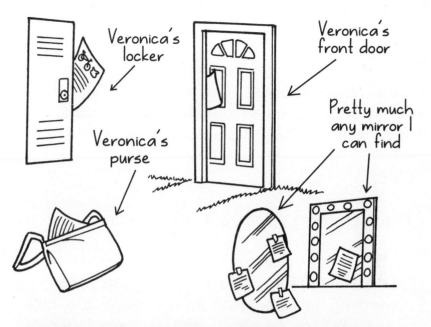

It seemed that my plan worked! I overheard Veronica and the Glossies talking about it during lunch! They were all saying how awesome the contest sounded and how they were all going to enter!

But I soon realized they were totally MISTAKEN and were reading the flyer ALL WRONG!

It turns out there's a big makeup company called BMX, which stands for Beauty Max! THAT'S what they were so excited about!

UGH!!!

The last thing on my list was... Archie.

I COULD tell Veronica that if she got a BMX bike, Archie would be super impressed. Something tells me that she would buy a bike in the blink of an eye if she thought it would get Archie's attention.

But I just can't do it.

I CAN'T!!!

Because that's part of MY plan! I want to get a bike so I can learn tricks, but I also want an excuse to invite Archie over so he can try my bike out too!

Not only that, but when I become a famous BMXer and start showing up in magazines and on soda labels, Archie will be so AMAZED. He'll definitely want to date me, then!

But how am I supposed to do all that if I don't have any way of getting a BMX bike to practice on?

I'm DOOMED!!

I did find a used BMX video game and tried playing that for a while, but it's just not the same!

The other day I decided to wander over to the skatepark to see if anyone there had a BMX bike. Even if I can't have one, at least I can watch other people do tricks, right?

Well, guess who I saw there?
Reggie and ARCHIE!

Archie was skateboarding but Reggie HAD A BMX BIKE!!!!

I never knew!!!

He could even do some tricks!!

Reggie noticed me watching and asked if I wanted to try his bike out. Of course I WANTED to, inside.

One problem though... Archie was nearby and I felt totally nervous about it! What if I made a complete fool of myself?! What if I looked like I needed training wheels?!

But when Reggie offered to show me a couple tricks, I couldn't refuse!

(Plus, I was secretly hoping that Archie would get jealous seeing me get tips from Reggie!)

I was a little wobbly at first. I didn't have any of my protective gear with me, but Reggie let me use his helmet at least, and he even told me how to do a bunny hop!

It took a few tries, but I DID IT! I did a BUNNY HOP!!! Even Archie noticed!!

YEaaaHHH!!!!

I'll be a pro in NO TIME!!

After practicing with Reggie for a while, I even started doing a couple small jumps off a baby ramp! Ok, so maybe I only got a few inches of air, BUT STILL!

PROGRESS!

I could totally sense Archie watching me the whole time and maybe it made me a LITTLE bit cocky. I started showing off more as I got more comfortable.

I should have just stopped while I was still ahead...

I was trying to do a 180 off a halfpipe and I totally WIPED OUT!

It turns out, I broke my arm. IT HURT SOOOO BAD!!! But Archie rushed to my side to help, and even though I was in excruciating pain, I was still pretty thrilled to realize he cared.

My parents weren't too happy to hear about my accident and as my dad drove me to the hospital, he told me I wasn't allowed to do any more dangerous tricks.

That's fine by me! I'm DONE with being a BMXer! It's just TOO dangerous and I have a lot of things I want to accomplish in life without breaking any more bones!

Having a broken arm is no fun, but when I showed up to school the next day with a cast, everyone wanted to sign it! Well, almost everyone. Veronica didn't. Weirdly, I think she was actually JEALOUS! How ridiculous is THAT?

The best part was that Archie asked to sign my cast. And guess what he wrote?

"You're the next Davey Starr! Get Well Soon! XOXO."

You DO know what XOXO means, right? It means hugs and KISSES!

KISSES!!!!!!!

I never want to take this cast off.

♡ *Betty Cooper*

Halloween

Dear Diary,

Woo-hoo! My favorite time of the year is here! Halloween!

The best part about it is getting to dress up in crazy costumes, but getting free candy is definitely a close second.

Veronica and I have gone trick-or-treating together ever since we were 5 years old. We always go in her neighborhood because the people who live there are super rich and they spend a lot of money to compete with each other over who can make their house look the spookiest.

The rich people also give out the most candy. Sometimes you get some really awesome stuff!

High-end dark chocolate bars imported from Switzerland

Homemade caramel apples with white chocolate drizzle and candied walnuts

Salt Water Taffy from Atlantic City

Gummy Tarantulas the size of your hand!

Ronnie and I also like to coordinate what costumes we're dressing up in. (It's sort of a best-friend thing.) Previous years' costumes have included Spooky Porcelain dolls (We did that last year), Good Witch and Wicked Witch (Guess who was the evil one?), Mermaids (It was kind of hard to walk when trick-or treating...) and Melted Ice Cream Cones (don't ask).

As for this year, I came up with the PERFECT costume idea! Something we've never done before, and something NO ONE ELSE will think of! I thought of it when I was going through the photos on my phone and found the one of Veronica wearing the wig that night we were dancing around pretending to be in Yeti Thrill.

I couldn't WAIT to tell Veronica my idea to dress up as dancing Yetis! But I had to wait till I could do it in private because I didn't want any other kids stealing my idea. The problem is, she's CONSTANTLY around the Glossies these days, so getting her alone is tricky.

All day long I tried to find a chance to talk to her, and it was IMPOSSIBLE! I probably looked like some kind of creeper the way I was following her around all day.

Well, eventually I gave up and just went up to her while she was primping in front of her locker mirror with the Glossies, and I told her I needed to talk to her in private.

All the Glossies gave me evil looks, and Veronica made a big show of rolling her eyes and saying "What do you want now?"

I told her we were running out of time to discuss our costumes for this Halloween, and that I had the most awesome idea ever, but I couldn't tell her what it was just yet. You would THINK she'd be intrigued, but I could NOT believe her reaction!!

I began to feel seriously DEPRESSED. Is Veronica right? Are we really too old to dress up and go trick-or-treating? I thought I could do it until at LEAST junior year!

My dad tried to cheer me up, but he doesn't get it. He'll always think I'm a little girl.

When I told him that this Halloween was going to be the WORST ever, he said, "If you want to dress up, then you should! Veronica's just being a stick in the mud. Besides, where am I going to get candy to eat if you don't go trick-or-treating for me?"

I told him if he wants candy that bad, he could just buy it for 50% off the day after Halloween. That's what all the grown ups do. Then he seemed all depressed too.

I spent a few days trying to accept the fact that I wouldn't be dressing up and trick-or-treating this year. But when everywhere you look, you see Halloween stuff, it's a CONSTANT reminder of what you're missing out on! I couldn't even bring myself to watch my favorite Halloween movies, which I do every year.

Come to think of it, I think this is how the whole Goth thing got started: Teens were depressed about not being able to take part in Halloween. Which kind of freaks me out--what if I turn into a Goth too?!!

No way! I can't let that happen!!!

So I decided that rather than become a Goth, I would just go ahead with my plans to take part in Halloween. If people make fun of me for being too old, well, TOO BAD!!!!

As it turns out, though, I was getting all worked up over nothing. Apparently most of the kids in my year are still dressing up and going trick-or-treating.

At the bus stop one day, Jughead asked me what I was going to be.

I was totally surprised and asked him if he was dressing up and trick-or-treating this year. And he was all like, "Uh, YEAH. It's like the one time of year where it's acceptable to beg strangers for chocolate and candy. You think I would miss that?!

He even told me that Reggie was going trick-or-treating too. (Reggie was going to be in charge of the tricks and Jughead would be in charge of the treats. Why am I not surprised???)

So that made me feel MUCH better about

celebrating Halloween. But that still left me with the problem of not having Veronica to coordinate with. This would be my first Halloween without her. That'd just be SO WEIRD!

I mean, I COULD just pretend she's dressed up as an invisible ghost at my side, but somehow I don't think it'd be the same.

Maybe it's time to find a NEW best friend, someone who's not all busy trying to grow up super fast. I could try asking Midge, but she and Moose are joined at the hip, and they always do some cute couple's costumes. Last year they were a princess and knight in shining armor.

After thinking about it a while, I decided that maybe Ginger Lopez could be my new BFF. True, I haven't hung out with her a whole bunch, but that would change once we decided to be besties! And really, she'd be PERFECT to dress up with. She's really fashionable and makes a lot of her own clothes, so her skills could come in quite handy for what I have in mind!

When I saw her in gym class, I decided to ask if she wanted to go in with me on my AWESOME costume idea.

But she told me that she was already working on Greek Goddess costumes for her and her best friend.

Dang! She already has a best friend, too. She WAS nice enough to invite me to be a Greek Goddess with them, but I'm kind of set on my own idea.

Next, I decided to ask Kumi, who moved here from Japan. She's kind of quiet, because she doesn't speak English super well, but sometimes you just have to become BFFs with someone in order to get past their shyness.

But then SHE was all like "Oh, Ginger and I are already dressing up together. Sorry!"

Ginger's her BFF?! Dang!!

Well so much for that. Last, I decided to ask Ethel. She's a little weird, but Halloween is all about being weird right? At first she seemed interested, but when I told her my idea to dress up as the yetis from Yeti Thrill, she turned me down!!!

She said she doesn't like that movie and asked if we could dress up like the space soldiers from Star Slugs instead.

I pretty much had to tell her "NO WAY! I don't like THAT movie!"

It looks like I'll just have to go solo with my costume this year...

Making a full-fledged Yeti costume is no easy feat! Do you realize how many yards of fabric it takes? I went to the fabric store to see what my options were and realized faux fur is NOT cheap. Especially the soft, silky kind that I wanted to use for my costume.

And what's worse, Veronica came into the fabric shop while I was there. Of course, she knew exactly why I was there and made fun of me for buying fake fur.

Really, Betty? You're going through with this Halloween business? What are you going to be, a werewolf? Hahaha!

I asked her why SHE was in the fabric store and she told me she was picking up designer silks and fabrics to have an evening dress custom-made. Of course, that just made me feel even more stupid and childish. UGH!!!

Anyway, I left the fabric shop empty-handed so I had to think of another way to make my costume.

I ended up using a shag rug we had in the basement. It smelled a little funky, but my mom said I could go ahead and use it, as long as I promised not to jam her sewing machine.

OK, so maybe I jammed her machine. But I have to say I'm still pretty impressed with my costume-making skills.

In fact, I'm beginning to think that maybe I'm meant to be a costume designer when I grow up. Think about it! I could get a job working on set for the ACTUAL Yeti Thrill movies! And I would get to dress the main actor Fletcher Collins, who is SO GORGEOUS!!!

So anyway, I FINALLY finished my costume! It's a little bulky and hard to move in, but it looks pretty awesome if I do say so myself!

The night before Halloween, I practiced Yeti Thrill dance moves and poses, because people give you more candy when you act the part!

I even made a matching fur bag to hold all my candy! It blends in with my costume so bullies like Reggie will have a harder time stealing my swag! (Like he did back in third grade--I'll NEVER forget!!!)

I was SO excited to go trick-or-treating, but when I was about to head out, my parents stopped me and demanded to know who I was trick-or-treating with. When I told them I was flying solo this year, they told me I couldn't go alone! Can you believe it?! I'm in high school and they still treat me like a little kid! UGH!!

So I had to go next door and ask if I could go with Jughead and Reggie. Jughead said it was fine, but I'd have to give him 10% of my treats as payment! Seriously?! Then, to add insult to injury, he said "What are you supposed to be anyway? A werewolf?"

Jughead was dressed as a giant treat bag because he said that way he could hold even more candy, and Reggie was a pirate AGAIN.

I swear, that's the only costume he owns.

All the better to play dastardly tricks on people!

Yar har har!

It's better than your scurvy costume!

At first I was annoyed at having to be stuck with these guys, but guess who ended up joining us? That's right, ARCHIE!! He was dressed as a star soldier from Star Slugs. And he even guessed what my costume was!

Hey!

Yeti Thrill!

And you're from Star Slugs, right? I LOVE that movie!

I guess trick-or-treating with other people wouldn't be so bad after all!!!

I told the guys that we should walk over to Veronica's neighborhood since the candy there is so much better. Reggie didn't want to walk that far, but Jughead and Archie were all about it!

Woo hoo! I was also secretly hoping that Veronica would see me trick-or-treating with Archie and having an awesome time, and would regret blowing me off!

Everywhere I went, my costume was a HIT! Even though most people thought I was trying to be a werewolf, they still gave me extra candy for doing a Yeti Thrill dance!!

But you won't believe it--at one point as we were making the rounds of the neighborhood, I saw another Yeti Thrill costume down the street! What the heck?! Did someone overhear my idea and steal it? If it was Ethel, she would have some MAJOR explaining to do!

I tried to catch up with the other Yeti and I couldn't help but notice how AWESOME their costume was. There's NO WAY they could be mistaken for a werewolf. They had amazing, silky, sparkly fur and everything!

In other words, their costume made my costume look totally lame. I then decided not to talk to them after all--they'd probably just make fun of me for how amateurish I looked compared to them. It also made me realize that maybe being a costume designer isn't the right job for me after all. Sigh...

Meanwhile, Reggie started complaining that our night had been too much about treats, and not enough about tricks.

Reggie is such a CHILD! His idea of trick-or-treating is to go up to other kids and demand a portion of their candy. If they refuse, he steals their masks or plays some other mean trick on them!

I ended up telling him I wanted nothing to do with it and was gonna go off on my own. Reggie got all mad and yelled, "This is what we get for letting a GIRL come trick-or-treating with us! Come on, guys, let's GO!"

But to my relief, Archie stood up for me and said he was gonna stick with me!!!! Even Jughead was like, "Betty's dances are getting us WAY more candy than bullying kids will!"

Oh, man! You should have seen the look on Reggie's face. He yelled "Traitors!" and stormed off on his own.

GOOD RIDDANCE!

It wasn't long before our treat bags were almost completely full. Jughead began to realize the problem with his costume was that he could hardly walk with so much candy stuffed into it.

We were about to decide to head back when we heard a commotion down the street. That's when we saw Reggie trying to get a kid to hand over their candy. Only, it wasn't just any kid--it was the other Yeti from earlier!! They wouldn't speak, and just ignored Reggie, which I think made him even more upset.

He was jumping up and down and yelling, "Hey, furball! Didn't you hear me? I said TRICK-OR-TREAT! Now hand over the goods, or else!"

Well, they STILL ignored him, which I thought was pretty cool. Finally Reggie got to see that not everyone is scared of him and his stupid tricks!

But would Reggie let it go? NOOO! He decided to go ahead and try and pull off the other yeti's mask. I knew I had to do something! Us yetis have to stay together!!

So I rushed forward and tried to stop him, and Reggie yelled, "Mind your own business, Betty!"

It turned into a big, chaotic wrestling match. Reggie trying to grab the mask, me trying to grab Reggie, and candy was just flying EVERYWHERE! Chaos, I tell you!

Despite my efforts, Reggie managed to pop off the other yeti's mask. And you will NOT believe who it was!!!!

Of course, Reggie has a crush on her, so he seemed to regret being such a bully and tried to make it seem like it was just a big joke.

Ronnie, I had no idea it was you! You're not mad, right? It was just fun and games, that's all! Besides, you're so beautiful, why would you cover up your lovely face?!

Shut up, Reggie!

As for me, I couldn't believe Veronica went trick-or-treating after all! And without me! Why didn't she just tell me?

It turns out, Veronica was embarrassed because the Glossies would kick her out of their clique if they knew she wanted to go trick-or-treating. That's why she made a costume with a mask--so no one would know it was her! And THAT'S what she was doing in the fabric store that day!

I was mad at first, but Veronica told me she was sorry and said, "I should have just told you. It would have been more fun to go trick-or-treating with you."

I said, "Well, look on the bright side. We're still matching, like we do every year!"

We decided to do one last round of trick-or-treating before heading home. With both of us doing a dance routine together, we got the MOST CANDY EVER!! I think Jughead was about to pass out from excitement.

Yeah, I think I'm going to keep doing this Halloween thing as long as I can!

♡ Betty Cooper

Spying

Dear Diary,

I never thought I would find myself saying this, but I think MAYBE I overdid it on the Halloween candy.

A few days after Halloween, I hadn't even gotten through half of my stash (383 pieces), when I came down with a massive stomach ache.

I told my mom that I suspected one of my candy pieces was poisoned, but she told me I was being a hypochondriac and that I just ate way too much at once.

Is this what getting older means? That you can't eat as much candy as you used to?!!

In any case, there was no way I could go to

school in my state, so I stayed home sick. I was forced to break my record of PERFECT ATTENDANCE at high school so far!!!

Man! I really wanted to get perfect attendance again this year. I don't know how they do things in high school, but in middle school they gave out trophies at the end of the year for the PAs (Perfect Attendees). I think they had a hard time picking a trophy that implied good attendance, so they used one that looks suspiciously like a track trophy. Now every time someone sees my trophies arranged on my dresser, they automatically assume that I'm some big-time marathon runner.

I'm not about to correct them, because who knows. I may grow up to be a marathoner! I mean, getting paid just to RUN? That's a pretty sweet deal, if you ask me.

Unfortunately, I'm currently in no shape to run anywhere, except to the bathroom every 10 minutes!!!

As if getting a stomach bug wasn't bad enough, my immune system was compromised and I ended up getting strep throat too and had to get antibiotics from a doctor. So even when I started feeling better, I had to stay home a few more days because I was too CONTAGIOUS!

Goodbye, trophy.

So I couldn't go to school even though I was feeling better, and I was still confined to the house like some kind of ZOMBIE!! You would think being home on a school day could be fun, but without being able to go out, I began to get totally stir crazy!

My mom heard me complaining and said that if I was bored, I could sort through my closet for donations to give to the charity truck that comes around once a month. Just like her to put me to work when I'm SICK!

But to be honest, I was a little curious to go through all my old stuff. My closet's gotten a little out of control in the last couple years... I'm not even sure what all might be buried in there anymore!

Man, I have so much STUFF! I began to feel like an archaeologist going on an excavation!

I think I've finally cracked through the top layer!

Come to think of it, being an archaeologist could be a pretty cool job. I should look into that.

After a couple hours, I hadn't even gotten to the back corners of my closet. Ok, so maybe I was getting a LITTLE distracted by some of the stuff I was finding, such as a Mall Maze board game that Ronnie got me for my 10th birthday, a watercolor set that I don't think I've ever actually used, and my old stuffed elephant, Tubbers!

My mom came up to check on my progress. She looked around and asked me where my donation pile was.

And I was like, "Ummmm..."

The problem was, I forgot I had such COOL stuff and I didn't actually WANT to get rid of any of it! But my mom wouldn't accept that. She pretty much told me I HAD to clean out my closet and start getting rid of stuff. GEEZ!!!

I tried really hard to start parting with stuff. But it wasn't easy!!

An old DVD

A hair scrunchie

A broken fashion doll

A mini desk fan

Then I rediscovered the COOLEST thing I forgot I had! An old SPY KIT! I can't believe I ever let it get so buried under all that other junk! It came with a bunch of cool stuff, like an Official Spy Badge (do spies even WEAR badges??), binoculars with a night vision switch, a laser pointer, a spy log notebook with coded paper and a decoding lens, and a voice-scrambling microphone!!!

Yeah, yeah, I know it's for little kids, but it was still awesome to find! I can't believe I never used any of this stuff before!

The coder paper and lens were kind of lame, but the voice scrambler really did make my voice sound all whack, especially since the batteries were dying.

But the best part were the binoculars! I could totally do some sweet bird watching with these! I decided to start right away and use the coded paper as my bird-sighting log.

Looking out my window, I didn't see any birds, though. Just Jughead's room. In fact, I saw WAY more of his room than I think I wanted to. I'm talking hamburger wrappers, empty drink cups and pizza boxes everywhere, along with video game controllers and action figures. It's SUCH a boy's room.

I went into the living room to look out the window that faces the back yard. Bird central!

But all I saw was a crow. And I think somehow he KNEW I was looking at him. It made me a little uncomfortable, to be honest.

I was making a note of this in my spy log/
bird book, when I was distracted by some
movement at the house behind ours. That's
where the creepy old lady Matilda Withers lives.

All the neighborhood kids call it the Haunted
House because it looks so much spookier than
all the other houses on the block. The lady
has GARGOYLES for crying out loud!

Most of us just steer clear of that place.
It used to freak me out that she lives right
behind my house, but pretty much keeps to
herself for the most part.

Anyway, I decided to take a peek in my
binoculars and see what was going on over
there, and I saw that she was in her backyard,
setting some kind of trap over a plate of
kibble!

Well, of course, this got my attention. What
could she be trying to catch? I assumed

maybe an annoying raccoon or something.

I decided I'd better keep an eye on it, and decided I would also use my coded spy notebook to log my observations about Miss Wither's house.

While I waited to see what she was trapping I also saw a couple finches hanging around outside.

OK, I thought there would be more birds than that! RIGHT? Hmm... Maybe I need to set out food or traps or something? (Is that what you're supposed to do if you're a birdwatcher?) I have no idea!

But maybe Miss Withers is a professional birdwatcher and she's trying to catch some rare bird. That would be pretty cool.

Well, it wasn't long before a cat strayed into her yard and got caught in the trap! I thought surely this was a mistake and that maybe I should see about setting it free, but then Miss Withers came out, grabbed the cat, and brought it inside. Maybe her cat just got lost...

But then she went and set the trap AGAIN! What the heck?

I noticed the curtains were open on one of her windows, so I decided to take a quick peek with with my binoculars and realized her house is full of cats!! Cats EVERYWHERE!!!!!

No wonder there's no birds outside. All of her cats must be eating them!! Geez!

The next day, I was well enough to go to school, but all I could think about all day were the cats that Miss Withers was trapping and bringing into her house.

I was almost certain: Riverdale has a CAT BURGLAR on their hands!!

But before I alerted any authorities, I decided I needed to confirm my findings and collect more evidence.

After school I snuck into her yard so I could take a closer look. I know TECHNICALLY that's called trespassing. But spies don't care about breaking the rules! That's what being a spy is all about! I may end up deciding that this is what I want to do with my life, so I better start practicing now, right?

Sure enough, I saw her cat trap set out (in fact, there was more than one!!)

And when I peeked through her window, I saw all her cats--and some were in CAGES!!! How cruel!!

I made sure to take some photos of the evidence so far.

But I think the most disturbing thing was when I smelled something and followed the scent around the house to where Miss Withers' kitchen is. When I peeked through the window, you will NOT believe what I saw!

She was baking pies like crazy! This could only mean one thing...

Suddenly, Jughead showed up and scared the living daylights out of me.

He told me he was lured there by the smell of baking pies and followed his nose to see what was cooking.

I pulled Jughead down and told him everything: how Miss Withers was trapping cats and bringing them into her house, keeping some in cages, and then baking them into pies!

It totally bummed Jughead out! He said "Even I wouldn't stoop so low as to eat a cat pie."

We had to tell someone!!

Jughead and I went to alert the authorities and found a policeman on patrol nearby. I told him the situation. But he didn't believe us!

He was just like, "Miss Withers? She's a lovely lady! I've had her pies, definitely no cats in there. Besides, you kids shouldn't be snooping on other people's property. That's trespassing! Blah, Blah, Blah."

He did tell us he would look into it, but he was laughing as he drove off so somehow I DOUBT IT!!

Since the policeman just thought we were making stuff up, we decided we had to go to someone who would actually CARE! Cat people!

Specifically, the Riverdale Cat Sanctuary. But when we got there, they were closed with a sign that they were getting ready for a Cat Convention that weekend. I have no idea what a Cat Convention is, but I decided I'd better attend so I could warn everyone.

The flyer said there would be food, so Jughead said he'd come too as backup.

Turns out the convention was a pretty big deal.
It was HUGE and lots of people were there!
All the better to warn everyone about Miss
Withers, the local cat burglar!

I was like, "Where's the PA system?" but
Jughead was just like, "Where's the FOOD?"

There was no getting Jughead to focus while
he was hungry so I agreed to find food with
him, only if he promised to help me find the PA
system so I could alert everyone there.

It was pretty easy to find the food area. We just had to follow his weirdly amazing sense of smell. But then you will NOT believe who we saw!!

Miss Withers at a booth, selling PIES to cat lovers!!!

I freaked out. Even Jughead said, "I never thought I'd say this... but I think I just lost my appetite."

That was IT. We needed to warn people! Just when someone was about to walk off with a pie, I had to jump in and say something.

Everyone just stopped and stared at me, waiting for an explanation. This was my chance to reveal all!

So I said, loud and clear, "Miss Withers has been luring and trapping cats to bake into her pies!"

And you know what happened? They started laughing at me. LAUGHING!!! Even Miss Withers was laughing!

It turns out I completely misread the entire situation. I was SO embarrassed when Miss Withers explained it.

She said, "I sell fruit pies to raise money for my practice. I trap feral cats that have no chance of living peacefully in a home, so I can have them vaccinated and neutered or spayed. Then I release them back into the wild. It's true I also have a lot of cats of my own, but I would never EAT them! My goodness!"

Oh.

So yeah. I felt pretty stupid after that and realized that I'm not really cut out to be a spy after all. Better keep looking for another thing to be when I grow up.

But Miss Withers wasn't mad at me. In fact, she gave both me and Jughead a pie to take home. Jughead was so excited, he didn't even wait to get home to eat it.

And I have to admit, the pie was pretty good. I even brought some home for my mom and dad, but it wasn't enough to distract my mom from asking me if I ever finished sorting my donatable items.

Turns out, I had a better idea for what to do with all my old stuff. I held a yard sale!

My mom did not approve. She was like, "Betty, the point of creating a donation pile was to give to charity--not profit from it!"

But I told her not to worry. I had a plan!

I made so much money! I had no idea so many strangers would be so willing to buy all my old junk!

But not everyone was a stranger. A few kids from school stopped by. In fact, Chuck Clayton stopped by and bought my spy kit, binoculars and all. And he paid good money for it too!

When my yard sale was over, there was just one thing left for me to do!

I went straight to Miss Withers' place and handed her a check and told her I was sorry for what I said the other day. I said I wanted to donate the proceeds from my yard sale to her cause.

Well, she was really happy and gave me a big hug and a pie to take home.

I guess she's not as scary of a person as I assumed. I mean, she's still a LITTLE weird. But aren't we all?

And, best of all, now I've got the hookup for awesome fruit pies!

♡ Betty Cooper

Extracurricular Activities

Dear Diary,

I know I'm just a freshman, and I MAY be getting a little ahead of myself, but I was reading up on how to get into a good college. Of course, before long I began to panic a little, because not only do you need good test scores and internships and stuff, but they also want to see that you've been active in "extracurricular activities."

As if I weren't busy enough with homework and trying to have a LIFE, now I need to figure out some extracurricular things to do on the side as well! The pressure is ON!

Still, I guess it's a good thing I found out about this now, so I have time to do all kinds of things before I graduate! Thanks to this insider knowledge, I'll be WAY ahead of everyone else by the time senior year rolls around!

OVER-ACHIEVER

I decided to go around the school and look for clubs seeking members and join as many as possible! I saw a poster advertising a Chess Club and marked that down as an option. I mean... I've never played chess before... but how hard can it be?

By the end of the day, I successfully signed up for SIX clubs--one for every day of the school week, plus one weekend club! Sure it might SOUND like a lot, but think of how good that will look on my college applications!

First up was Movie Club on Mondays. This club seemed pretty rad--all you do is WATCH

MOVIES, and then talk about them. It doesn't get much easier than that! (Maybe this extracurricular stuff will be way easier than I thought.)

Raj Patel was the club leader, and he's a big film buff, so I figured it'd be cool.

I asked him if we'd be watching any of the Yeti Thrill movies. He gave me a weird look and said "Um, no. We'll be watching REAL movies about REAL issues."

The first movie that we watched was some French black and white film called "Larmes d'un Clown" which means "Tears of a Clown." Is it me, or does that sound like a straight up HORROR film?? But it wasn't scary at all!

In fact, I honestly did NOT know what was going on half the time. Except at one point there was an actual clown crying on a street corner.

And HOW does this have to do with "REAL life issues," exactly?

The discussion afterward was equally as confusing.

Raj said something fancy like, "I felt the clown as a symbol of laughter was a poignant juxtaposition with the sorrow of losing his balloon."

And some other smarty-pants student said, "It makes you ponder the temporality of life. The balloon itself is a metaphor for dreams, and their futility."

I said, "Well, I thought the clown was kind of random and freaky. Like they wedged it in just because of the movie title."

Let me just say no one seemed to appreciate my remarks.

So maybe my other clubs would work out to be better.

Tuesday was Glee Club, which sounded cool because I love watching shows about singing and dancing.

But, unfortunately, I'm not really good at either. Mostly, I just lip synced when we sang in groups, so no one could hear how bad I sounded. And the choreography was HARD!

I thought that because I can do the Yeti Thrill moves that this would be a cake walk.

WRONG!

Wednesday's Chess Club wasn't much better.

Uhhhh...How does the horsey move again?

We're trying to prepare for an important tournament! You need to learn more quickly!

Hmph! Maybe I should start my own club where EVERYONE is welcome and isn't made to feel like an IDIOT for being there.

Thursday I had Book Club. Another easy one-- or SO I THOUGHT!

Apparently, they read a new book every WEEK! I mean, I LOVE to read, but who has time to read that quickly? Especially when SOME of us have 5 other clubs? And go figure, this week's book is as thick as my arm--a high fantasy spanning generations and featuring approximately a million characters!

Friday was Soccer Club, which I actually kind of enjoyed. But the problem was, I was so exhausted from the first four clubs, I didn't play very well.

I was beginning to think I wasn't cut out for ANY club. Which made me think that maybe

I'm not good at ANYTHING. What college will want someone like me? I still don't know what I want to do when I grow up--I can't even pick a club!

But I couldn't lose hope... I still had one club left--Riverdale High Newspaper Club, which meets on Saturdays at the local library.

Things were looking up when I learned that Archie is in this club. In fact, he writes all the articles about our school's sporting events! So when the club leader, Kevin Keller, said he needed someone to be a photographer for the sports section, I jumped at the chance (literally), and cried "I'LL DO IT!!!!"

Yeah, I got shushed by some old lady in the library. Oh, well. It was worth it.

The problem is... I don't have a camera. I mean, I DO have a camera on my phone, but that's not good enough if I'm going to be a PROFESSIONAL newspaper photographer! Of course, I didn't tell Kevin this, but I knew I had to figure something out ASAP!

My mom has a fancy camera--maybe she'd let me use it??? But when I asked her, she didn't seem so sure.

I guess she doesn't TRUST me with her expensive things, which is totally insulting! Just because I jammed her sewing machine and wrecked her yoga mats, and accidentally spilled soda all over her laptop when I was in seventh grade, doesn't mean I'm going to mess up her camera! I'm not USUALLY that careless! Geez!

Still, despite all that, she said I could borrow it if I did some extra chores around the house. Great. ANOTHER thing to add to my already packed schedule. Better work on my multitasking!!!!

HOMEWORK!

So the camera my mom lent me is SUPER COOL. But it's also SUPER COMPLICATED. There are so many knobs and buttons that I don't know what any of them do yet. I asked my mom to show me how to use it, but she told me I would learn better by experimenting and she handed me the manual for reference.

The manual is about as thick as "Claim to the Throne"!!! I don't have time for this!!!!!

Well, if experimenting is the quickest way to learn something, then that's what I'll do!

After school one day, I asked Archie if I could take a couple test photos of him to make sure my camera settings were right... The way I see it, it's like killing two birds with one stone: I'll be learning how to use my camera AND I'll have secret photos of him all for myself! (Ronnie would flip out if she knew I had a secret stash of Archie photos to drool over.)

Unfortunately my efforts to take his portrait were pretty much a huge fail. In some of the pics, I framed the photo weird and basically decapitated him!! In some others, he was all blurry, and then some were way too dark. Ugh!!!

OK, so that didn't work out. But I'm not going
to give up yet. I'll have plenty more chances
to get photos of Archie when we're covering
sporting events!

In the meantime I decided I would keep
practicing by taking photos during all my other
clubs.

Speaking of all my clubs, I am getting
SERIOUSLY overwhelmed! I have to overlap
them just to keep up!

That means secretly reading my Book Club
book during Movie Club...

Memorizing chess moves during Glee Club...

Thinking of soccer strategy during Book Club...

And singing Glee Club songs during my chores!

I am SO EXHAUSTED!!! But at least taking photos of all my various clubs has helped me figure out the camera enough that I'm able to take proper photos now!

Now if I could just stay awake during the sporting events I have to go to AFTER all my clubs.

How am I going to keep this schedule up for four years of high school? I'd better get into EVERY college I apply to for this!!!!

Even though it's really tough to keep up with everything, getting to hang out with Archie for Newspaper Club is SO WORTH IT!

Not only that, but my photo taking skills are getting way better! Check out some doodles of my favorite shots:

In fact, I'm beginning to think that maybe this is what I'm meant to do when I grow up. I can go all over the world taking photos of stuff for magazines and newspapers! I could have gallery shows and sell my portraits for millions!

Anyway, I thought I had everything under control with all my clubs and responsibilities, but then everything started to fall apart HORRIBLY!

It started when Veronica got mad at me for not having time to hang out with her after school. I tried explaining that I had six clubs PLUS sporting events I had to attend. You'd THINK she'd be understanding, but nooooo!

It turns out Veronica has a Fashion Design Club, and she wanted me to join or ELSE. The problem is, it's at the same time as Chess Club. I wasn't sure how I was going to be in two places at the same time!!!

But it turns out I didn't have to worry about it, because I was BOOTED from Chess Club when we had a mini tournament against Greendale and I forgot how to set up my board.

Dilton was pretty upset with me...

But Dilton said chess is all about performing well under stress and that I wasn't taking it seriously. UGH!

Then Veronica's Fashion Design Club wasn't much better because the Glossies were in it! I should have known!

When I was walking in, one of them was like, "Betty, I think you're in the wrong club."

And the other one said, "Yeah, this is for people who know what fashion is!"

And the last one was all, "Go back to your dorky Chess Club where you belong!"

Then Veronica said, "Don't be mean, guys. She got kicked out of Chess Club!"

I wish she hadn't told them that!!! They would NOT stop laughing at me!

Just when I didn't think things could get any worse, they DID.

I was trying to get more action shots during Soccer Club (since I'm supposed to be shooting sporting events anyway), but I got a little TOO close to the action.

My nose got bruised, but I didn't even care about that because I BROKE MY MOM'S CAMERA!!!! She was going to be FURIOUS with me, I just knew it!!

Luckily, the memory card in the camera was still ok, so I was able to hand Kevin all my photos at the next Newspaper Club meeting.

But I couldn't believe it when he said he couldn't use ANY of them for the school newspaper.

He said the problem was that Archie was in EVERY single photo I took. He said, "We just can't have a newspaper full of Archie!"

I didn't realize... I told him I didn't do it on purpose!

I was SO embarrassed. And Archie must think I'm a total CREEP! All this club stuff has turned out to be a DISASTER!!! It's clear I'm not good at ANYTHING! I'll never get into a good college, so WHY BOTHER?!

I decided to just go home and have a pity party.

I wanted to just lock myself in my room for eternity, but when my mom got home from work, I knew I had to tell her I broke her camera. I was NOT looking forward to her reaction. I was certain she would completely flip out and start yelling at me.

But instead she said, "OK, so what are you going to do about it?"

I was like, "I don't know! I said I was sorry!"

My mom said I had to take responsibility for my actions. I told her I got into this whole mess BECAUSE I was trying to be responsible by signing up for so many extracurricular activities, but I basically failed at all of them.

She told me that responsibility isn't about biting off more than you can chew. It's about having integrity and following through with your actions. She also said if I was getting overwhelmed, it'd actually be more responsible to cut back instead of letting people down.

I realized that by not focusing 100% on each club, and by trying to multitask, I wasn't being very responsible after all...

I decided to drop out of some of my clubs and apologize to the leaders for letting them down. It wasn't easy, but I felt better afterward.

(And WAY more relaxed!)

Still, I wasn't sure how to go about fixing my mom's camera. There was no way I could afford to have it replaced or even fixed--those things are EXPENSIVE!!!

I tried duct taping it, but it just looked kind of janky. I better figure something else out...

Back to the drawing board...

Anyway, I was feeling pretty bummed until Kevin showed up at my locker one day.

Turns out, I REALLY had fun writing the article about all the clubs. Hmm... maybe I'm meant to be a writer or journalist! This could be my TRUE CALLING!

Kevin really liked the article too--he even put it on the FRONT PAGE!

Before I knew it, all the leaders of the clubs

I joined were coming up to thank me for writing such a good article! I even mentioned Veronica's Fashion Design Club (AND held back from saying anything snarky about the Glossies!)

Even Dilton was happy! During lunch, he came up to me to thank me for putting the Chess Club on the front page!

He told me that ever since the newspaper came out, the Chess club has had a 164% jump in membership. He also said sorry for getting so frustrated with me earlier and said if there was anything he could do to make it up to me, he would.

SOOOO, I got Dilton to help me fix my mom's camera. And I even learned a little about it in the process!

Afterwards, the camera was like new again and my mom was happy. She said she was proud of me for taking responsibility!

So basically, I've learned my lesson. It's better to do a few things really well rather than a lot of things poorly. And I've learned that being a photographer is NOT for me.

BUT! I'm still happy with the photos I took. Maybe they couldn't be used for the newspaper, but I wasn't about to let them go to waste!

♡ Betty Cooper

Field Trip

Dear Diary,

Last week, my history class went on a field trip to the museum! I didn't know we'd still get to go on field trips in high school, so I was SO excited! Our teacher, Mr. Clayton (Chuck's dad), wanted us to see this new traveling mummy exhibit at the museum.

(And by traveling mummies, I mean it's an exhibit that's being shown at museums around the country, not literally traveling mummies. Although that would be pretty rad.)

We all took a bus to the museum. I wanted to sit by Archie, but Veronica beat me to the punch, so I was stuck next to Chuck who was SO embarrassed because his dad kept making bad puns about "wrap-stars" the whole way there.

When we got to the museum, it was SO crowded. I think every school in the area decided to have a field trip there that day-- there were kids running around everywhere, screaming and being obnoxious. Man, I'm so glad I'm in high school now--I don't remember being that annoying when I was little.

I have to say, the mummy exhibit was pretty impressive. They decorated an entire wing to look like an Egyptian pyramid... it was a little spooky! Especially since they had cases filled with ACTUAL ancient mummies from thousands of years ago!

I couldn't help but imagine what it'd be like to be in the museum after-hours when it's all dark and empty. Freaky deeky!

We were given digital headsets to listen to recordings about each piece in the exhibit. I was totally interested in hearing the audio tour, but I think half the students in my class didn't even bother turning theirs on. Veronica was obsessed with pointing out all the jewelry she'd want for her own collection, and she kept interrupting my audio tour to show me every little thing she liked.

I couldn't help but notice that Archie was busy listening to his audio tour too. I tried to time mine so I could stay next to him as much as possible. So... maaaybe I had to skip a couple of the exhibits to make it line up with his.

Exhibit five, pottery shards from-- BEEP! Exhibit six-- palm fr--BEEP! Exhibit seven, Queen Nefertiti.

But then my audio tour broke down! It got all messed up and garbled!

I definitely needed a replacement set. I was going to ask Mr. Clayton, but he was busy yelling at Reggie for being disruptive. (Shocker.)

Rather than interrupt, I decided to just go back to the museum entrance and replace the audio set myself. No big deal, right?

WRONG!

Some jerk security guard blocked me from going back into the exhibit!!! He asked me for my ticket and when I told him I had already been inside he said, "No re-entry! If you want to go in again, you need to buy another ticket."

I told him my class was still inside but he was unmoved by my pleas. And of course, I didn't have any money with me to buy another ticket!

So that meant I was stuck outside the exhibit AND worried about getting in trouble for splitting up from the group. UGH!

Well, if I wasn't able to get back into the exhibit, I decided I might as well make the most of my exile by checking out the rest of the museum. I mean, if I was gonna get in trouble for ditching the group, I might as well have some fun doing it, right?

Naturally, the first place I went to see was... The Dinosaur Wing! I felt like I was visiting old friends.

After I finished learning everything I need to know about dinosaurs, I went over to the next wing, which has Native American art and some really awesome totem poles.

Seeing all this cool stuff almost made up for missing out on the Egyptian exhibit... Almost.

I wondered if Archie and everyone else was having fun. I wondered if Mr. Clayton was still making bad puns, or if Reggie was still misbehaving. (Probably yes, yes, and yes.)

I tried to cheer myself up by going to one of my favorite parts of the museum--the mammal section with all the taxidermied animals posing against painted backdrops. My favorite one is the lions, mostly because the father lion looks sort of cross-eyed and confused, even though I think they were TRYING to make him look noble.

I totally freaked out when I heard a stuffed raccoon behind me make a noise. It sounded JUST like a kid crying!!!!

waaaaaaaaaaaHHHH!!!

Waahh!!

But, to my relief, I realized it wasn't a case of a dead raccoon making a horrible ghostly cry, but it was a little kid who was hiding behind the pedestal. She was crying because she got separated from her group too!

Of course I HAD to help! I asked her if she was lost, but all she could do was cry. REALLY LOUD.

Since she was so hysterical, I tried a different tactic. I told her I was lost too, and asked if she could help me find MY group. And that actually calmed her down and she said ok!

She told me her name was Violet and that she was in second grade. I figured it'd be pretty easy to find her class... I bet they were freaking out looking for her. (How did they even lose track of her in the first place?? Seriously!!! SO IRRESPONSIBLE!)

As we walked through the museum looking for her class, we ended up stopping at some of the exhibits and I even taught her a few things!

I have to say, not only am I good at being a babysitter, I'm also pretty good at being a teacher! Maybe THIS is what I'm supposed to do with my life. But which one? Hmm... I guess when you think about it, both are kind of similar. I could just combine the two!

Just as we were passing through the space exhibit, you will not believe who we ran into! Archie! He seemed a little flustered. I asked him what he was doing there and he said he noticed that I never got back from exchanging my headset, so he went to see where I was... but the guard wouldn't let him back inside either!

I acted cool about it, but inside I was doing cartwheels! Archie NOTICED I was gone!!! He even cared enough to come looking for me!!!

And now he's been exiled too! I mean, I felt a little bad about that, but still. If I was going to be stuck outside the exhibit, I'd rather be stuck with Archie!

Archie joined our hunt for Violet's class. We went through the aquatic exhibit next. The light was all blue and glowy, and sort of dreamy, and I caught Archie smiling at me when we walked by the life-size blue whale. It WOULD have been more romantic if Violet wasn't around.

I admit I was pretty relieved when we finally spotted Violet's class by the Kiddy Discovery Zone. (I think her teacher was also pretty relieved that she wouldn't end up getting sued for neglect.)

The teacher thanked us and gave us two spare tickets she had to a special rocks and gem exhibit upstairs. So naturally that's where Archie and I headed next!

The exhibit was really cool. Especially since no one was there and Archie and I had the WHOLE place to ourselves. We saw a MASSIVE geode!

Remember how I said the aquatic exhibit was romantic? Well it had NOTHING on the phosphorescent rocks section. There was a dark hallway filled with neon-colored glowing cave rocks. Although it was so dark that Archie tripped and fell and I almost fell right on top of him!

We ended up just sitting on the floor under the glowing rocks and it was probably the most romantic thing I've EVER experienced and for a minute I was CERTAIN I was about to get my first kiss.

Trust me, I TRIED to stay cool but my brain was running a million miles a minute, buzzing with a TON of concerns.

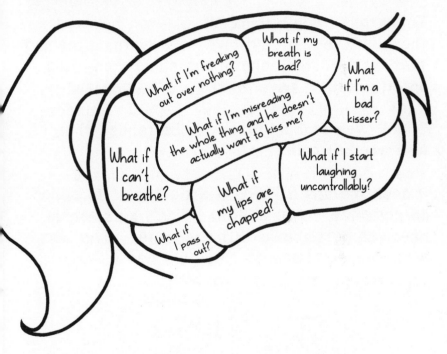

But--JUST MY LUCK--I'll never get to know if Archie was actually about to kiss me or not because a security guard came along and yelled at us for sitting in the hall!

He dragged us to the exit of the Egyptian exhibit where our class was just getting out,

and he embarrassed us in front of everyone!!!!
He told Mr. Clayton that he caught me and
Archie trying to make out in the rock exhibit
and OF COURSE everyone heard and was like
"OOOOOOOOOOHHHHH!"

Where the heck do they find these Riverdale
Museum guards? They're horrible!!

Thankfully I don't think Mr. Clayton believed
the guard, but he did give us a warning, saying
that we'd better behave ourselves from here
on out, or he'd have to tell our "mummies."

Chuck was probably more embarrassed than I
was at that point.

It took me the ENTIRE bus ride back to school
to convince Veronica that I didn't kiss Archie.
She was pretty livid. But the worst thing was
when we got back to class we had a POP
QUIZ about the Egypt exhibit!!

The thing is, I could have answered any question about dinosaurs, or Native American art, or mammals, or space, or aquatic life, or even geodes. But I didn't know anything about the Egypt exhibit. GO FIGURE!!

I guess the only good thing about getting a C on my quiz was that I ALMOST got my first kiss.

Or DID I???

♡ Betty Cooper

Band Practice

Dear Diary,

I had a super important science test to study for, but could I get any peace and quiet? NO! For the past week, every night after school, all I could hear was Jughead banging around on some drum set. I didn't even know he played drums (actually, I'm still not convinced he can.) UGH!!!

I tried to block out the sound by blasting my favorite music (Josie and the Pussycats) really loud, but then my mom got mad at ME for being too loud!!

My mom told me if I had a problem with Jughead, I needed to let him know instead of being "passive aggressive."

So finally, I HAD it, and stormed over to Jughead's house to give him a piece of my mind!

When he answered the door (holding a chicken drumstick in one hand and drum drumsticks in the other) I told him his CONSTANT drumming was interfering with my studies! He was all like, "You need to relax, Betty! Music is a great remedy, you know. I'm just practicing for a band me and Archie are forming and I've never felt more chill!"

And I was like, "HOW can you feel chill doing all that aggressive banging? Wait... did you say a band with Archie?"

I admit I was a bit intrigued! I had no idea Archie was musical!

Jughead even suggested that I join. He said they were still looking for a keyboardist, a

bassist and a singer. Of course, the idea
of being in a band with Archie is TOTALLY
awesome!

One problem: I can't play any instruments OR
sing!!

But I wasn't about to tell Jughead that. I
mean, how hard can it be to learn?

I was pretty sure there was some old keyboard
in the attic that I used to play with when I
was little, so I went up there to hunt for it.

I did find a kazoo, but I'm not sure that
counts as an instrument. Anyway, it tasted
kind of funny.

Finally I found the keyboard! It was buried under tons of junk AND I came across a spider, so it had BETTER be worth it!

But when I plugged it in and tried playing it, I realized half the keys didn't even work. And some of the keys that DID work made awful noises. Like, scary-awful.

I guess it sounded awful enough that my dad rushed into the attic thinking there was a wasp infestation.

But when my dad saw there weren't any wasps, and that I was looking for an instrument, he got all weird and happy-teary-eyed and said, "I never thought I'd see the day you were interested in playing an instrument! Do you remember how much of a tantrum you threw when we tried to sign you up for music lessons in third grade?"

I told him that was forever ago, and why did he care so much anyway?

My dad then went into a trunk and pulled out an old bass! I had no idea he had one! He said, "Didn't you know I used to be bit of a rocker in my day?"

And I was like, "Uhhhhh... No?"

I was kind of just hoping he would let me borrow his bass so I could start practicing but then he went on a rampage, looking for some old video of his college band, Screaming Phoenix.

When he finally found the tape, he spent forever hooking up a converter so he could show it to me on the computer. I swear I've never seen him so excited. When I finally saw the footage I wasn't quite sure WHAT to think...

I have to say, I felt kind of MORTIFIED seeing my dad like that. It almost made it worse that he was so proud of it, because it sounded TERRIBLE!

Even my mom walked in and was horrified.

She was like, "Oh, Hal. Not that!"

And he said, "Hey, you thought it was cool when you met me! Remember how you used to wait outside every show and--"

But my mom cut him off and told him that he had to let go of his past "obsession."

Drama!

Well, finally THAT was over with and my dad offered to start teaching me how to play bass. He started by showing me some basic notes. It was kind of tricky getting my hands to cooperate.

Then he got this misty look in his eyes and asked if maybe he and I could form a father-daughter band.

I can't say I really want to be in a band with my DAD, but I didn't have the heart to tell him I would rather be in Archie's band.

So I was kinda just like, "Um... sure, Dad."

But then he got really excited and cried, "Yess!! This will be great! We can make t-shirts and perform at open mic nights! Maybe work on an EP!"

Yikes.

Even with my dad's help, I decided if I REALLY want to learn bass, I better get some other resources, so I printed out a bunch of tutorials from online, and practiced learning to read notes and playing scales.

But when my dad saw what I was doing, he got all upset!

Seriously, WHAT has gotten into my dad? (He was even wearing a bandana, which is kinda weird, amiright?!!)

So, fine! If my dad wanted me to learn by "feeling the groove" or whatever, I decided the best way to learn would be to play along to some of my favorite music. So I blasted Josie and the Pussycats and tried to jam along to that. I think I started to get what my dad was saying about getting lost in the music.

In fact, I TOTALLY could imagine myself as a cool rocker chick. Maybe THIS is my true calling! I could perform at stadiums and festivals to tons of adoring fans!

I was really starting to get into it, but APPARENTLY my dad had a problem with my choice of music. He switched it off and was all, "What is this sugary junk, Betty? You need to learn from some true masters!"

He then proceeded to bombard me with all of HIS favorite music from the olden days!

Geez! I had no idea my dad was such a music snob!

The more we practiced together, the more I noticed my dad starting to revert back to his old rocker days. He started growing a BEARD and wearing studded jewelry.

I mean, it's great that he was reliving his youth or whatever, but did he have to go and EMBARRASS me while doing it?

Even my mom started to get concerned when, one morning while we were eating eggs, my dad said "Man! Forget this square meal! Let's order a pizza for breakfast!"

She told him "this" was getting out of hand.

My dad then accused my mom of "cramping his style" and went off to sulk in the garage.

I thought I was supposed to be the teenager here!

There was a reason your dad left the whole band thing behind the first time around. He gets obsessed! And he couldn't stop fighting with his bandmates, so they broke up. Honestly, I was relieved!

I can see why. I kind of wish I had my old dad back...

Things only got worse... My dad wanted to come up with a band name so he could design t-shirts, but we couldn't agree on anything!

Then he got mad when I had to miss practice to do homework! Can you believe it?! I TOLD you my dad was acting weird!

He got all whiny and said that we'd never be "ready" if we didn't practice. And I was like, "Ready for WHAT? Dad, I have a TEST tomorrow! That's what I need to be ready for!"

That sort of seemed to smack some sense into him. My dad apologized and said I was right. He even took off his bandana.

He said, "Of course school should come first... I don't know what came over me. I guess I just got so caught up in old memories..."

I said, "I know, Dad. And I hate to say it, but maybe our band should break up..."

I was really worried about my dad's reaction, but he took it pretty well.

You're right, it's for the best. You know I still love you though.

And we can still keep practicing together from time to time. I still want you to help me learn.

It's a deal.

After that, things got back to normal. I think my mom was really relieved too!

The next day I saw Jughead at the bus stop. He asked me how my bass was coming along, and asked if I was ready to come practice with him and Archie after school and help brainstorm band names.

Believe it or not, I had to turn him down. I told him I was practicing with my dad instead.

As much as I'd like to hang out with Archie more, I just got over one band breakup. I don't think I'm ready to do the whole band thing again just yet.

Besides, I have to get really good first, so I can impress everyone!

Then, watch out, world!

♡ Betty Cooper

Dance Planning

Dear Diary,

Great. Now I have a whole new thing to worry about. Homecoming is coming up and you know what that means.

I have to find a dress, and I have to find a DATE. And now that I'm in high school, dances are SERIOUS BUSINESS. In middle school our dances were called "socials."

No one ever danced at the socials, which is why I guess they decided to call them socials, and not dances. But no one really socialized either. They should have just called them "standings."

All the girls would stand on one side of the room waiting for the boys to ask them to dance, and all the boys would hang out on the other side, trying to act like they didn't want to be there. AWKWARD.

But now that I'm in high school, it's a whole new game. And I'd better be prepared! Of course, the minute Veronica heard about the dance, she joined the planning committee along with the Glossies. She takes dances more seriously than anyone I know.

Pen chewed from anxiety

Intense look of concentration

Binder stuffed to the gills

I just hope Archie doesn't ask her out instead of me. Having to watch them dance together all night would be TORTURE!!!

So now I just need to figure out a way to get him to ask me, because I KNOW Veronica will be totally trying to get him to ask her first. The other day Veronica cornered me in the hall and INSISTED very strongly that I join the planning committee. She said they NEEDED someone with my organizational skills, and that the dance was SUPER important, and if I was REALLY her friend, I'd help her out.

To be honest, I don't really NEED any more responsibility. And I wonder if Veronica wants me to join the planning committee just so she can keep tabs on me. Hmph!

Then again, she did offer to let me borrow one of her dresses which would be pretty awesome. So I said yes.

I don't think the Glossies were too happy to see that I joined.

They're SO RUDE. I don't know WHY Ronnie hangs out with them. I guess it's because she likes how they basically WORSHIP her, even though she's younger than them. (It's because she's so rich and wears all the latest designer clothing.)

Anyway, I didn't really WANT to be part of the planning committee at first, but once I got into it, I found I sort of liked it!

There's A LOT to take care of... decorations, music, food, ticket sales, and photographers. The list goes on. But Veronica was right—I AM good at organizing stuff! In fact, I'm so good at it, I wonder if I should become a professional party planner when I grow up. Then I could work with all kinds of celebrities and plan their fancy events and spend all their money on really cool things like ice sculptures and chocolate fountains.

Okay, send in the acrobats!

My favorite part of the planning is working on the posters for the event, which we get to hang ALL over the place. Since I'm the best artist in our group, it was my job to make all the posters.

This was PERFECT! Since I knew Archie would be seeing them, I decided to draw in subliminal clues to get him to ask me to the dance.

Blonde and Redhead Dancing (I tried not to make it look TOO much like us!)

Bumblebees in flowers (kind of random, but the more "B" words there are, the more Archie will think of "Betty")

Secret message hidden cleverly in the design (Just in case all the other symbolism doesn't work)

And Veronica had NO CLUE. She actually LIKED my posters! Well, for the most part. She asked me what was with all the bees. I told her they were just decorations!

The Glossies, on the other hand, did NOT like my posters. But I think that's mostly because they don't like ME. Whatever. They're just jealous of my mad art skills!

After all the posters were hung, I waited for Archie to notice and then ask me to the dance! But days and DAYS went by and I began to wonder if he even bothered LOOKING at my posters!

Some jerks also vandalized my posters outside the cafeteria! UGH!

When I saw Jughead at the bus stop, I decided to see if Archie maybe mentioned anything to him. But I had to play it cool--I didn't want him to know I was fishing for info! So I started by asking him if he saw all the posters for the dance around school.

And he said, "Yeah, but what's with all the bees?"

Would everyone just drop it about the bees already?! GEEZ! I decided to change the subject and asked if Jughead was planning to go to the dance.

Ugh, this was off to a BAD start. I can't believe Jughead thought I was asking HIM to the dance! Like THAT would ever happen!

So I tried to switch gears and just flat out asked him if he knew whether or not Archie was going to the dance or not.

ARRRRRRRGHH! Jughead can be SO annoying sometimes!

I decided I WOULD just ask Archie the next time I saw him. But when I DID see him next, I completely chickened out and couldn't form a proper sentence to save my LIFE!

He was like, "'Sup, Betty!"

And all I could manage was something like, "Har... my post... you... yeah?"

I must have looked like a complete IDIOT! I then had to pretend I was having an allergic reaction so I could use that as an excuse to run out of the room.

Yeah, I'm not proud of that.

I was really REALLY hoping Archie would forget all about that, but he's just so considerate! He saw me in the hall and asked me if I was ok.

I didn't have the heart to tell him that I was the one who drew the posters. I was already MORTIFIED enough as it was! And because I was so flustered, I even missed that perfect chance to ask him if he was going to the dance. I mean, he BROUGHT IT UP and I STILL failed to ask him!!!

MAJOR FAIL.

To release my frustration I went around to every poster I could find around school and crossed out all the STUPID BEES!

Maybe it's just as well that I didn't ask Archie if he was going to the dance. I may not have liked his answer. During one of our planning committee meetings, Veronica sort of turned it into a dressing-room extravaganza. Never mind that we still have about a MILLION things to do! I guess she thinks the ice sculpture will order itself?!?!

Anyway, she wanted to show us a few options for dresses for the dance. Naturally they were ALL expensive and they were ALL gorgeous. I was going along with her little show-and-tell until she said, "Girls, I think this might be the one! It will go best with Archiekins' hair color, don't you agree?"

Wait a minute! Did this mean Archie ALREADY asked Veronica to the dance? I tried to smile, but inside I felt like this:

I was SO bummed, I almost quit the planning committee right there and then.

But... I managed to stop myself from doing anything rash.

Because, seriously, WHO will order the ice sculpture if I don't?!

So instead I went home and listened to sad music.

Jughead was no help when I saw him the next day.

So? Did you ask Archie to the dance yet?

NO! MIND YOUR OWN BUSINESS!

I did feel a little bad for blowing up at him like that, so at lunchtime I gave him my pudding cup and all was forgiven. I guess I'm lucky to have a friend like Jughead, because he doesn't hold grudges like Veronica does!

But, of course, Veronica had to see me give Jughead the pudding cup and now she's convinced I have a CRUSH on him!!

She said that we should go to the dance together because we were perfect for each other and I was like, "What's THAT supposed to mean?!"

I keep telling her I'm not interested, but she will not let it DROP! She thinks I'm just being coy, and the more I argue, the more she thinks I'm trying to cover up my "true feelings"! I just CAN'T WIN!! UGH!

But Veronica DID keep her word and let me pick out one of her dresses to wear to the dance! So that was pretty cool.

I picked a shimmery green dress because it made me feel like a mermaid!

Veronica said, "Betty, this dress is PERFECT for you! And Jughead will LOVE it!"

I told her unless it was made of hamburgers, I doubt Jughead would notice any dress that any girl was wearing.

Not that I want him to notice, anyway!!

So at least I had the dress figured out, but that still leaves me with needing to find a DATE! But guess what?

GOOD NEWS! I found out Archie hasn't asked Veronica to the dance after all!

I found out when I was at Veronica's and we were doing our nails to match our dresses.

She told me Reggie asked her to the dance and that normally she'd say NO, but she was keeping him as a backup option because she was still waiting for Archie to "get his act together" and ask her.

I tried to act like the news was no big deal, but inside I was like:

And the best part? According to the color wheel, my green dress is a complimentary color to Archie's red hair! So Veronica is letting me wear the PERFECT DRESS and she doesn't even REALIZE it!

So, overall, things have been looking up!

Well, except for where the GLOSSIES are concerned.

They are really starting to get on my nerves! So far I've put up with their mean comments and their stuck-up attitudes and everything else, but my patience is running OUT!

On top of that, they hardly do ANY work in the planning committee. I'm pretty much the ONLY one getting things done! And do they show me any appreciation?

NO!

They just keep picking on me--especially when Veronica isn't around.

One of them was like, "So, Betty. Have you decided which thrift shop you'll be getting your dress at?"

And the other one said, "If you need to borrow a couple dollars, I'm sure we can ask our class to pitch in. You do take quarters, right?"

I couldn't help myself. I had to tell them that

Veronica was lending me one of her designer dresses. I hate to brag, but then again, the looks on their faces were PRICELESS.

They actually thought I was making it up! So I decided to SHOW THEM! Literally. The next day I brought the dress to school so they could see I was telling the truth.

You will NOT believe what happened next.

I was horrified! That beautiful dress--ruined!
I knew Veronica would FREAK OUT if she saw
the damage!

I was so mad, I knew I had to do something to
get back at them. And who better to ask than
Reggie?

After school, I caught up with him and told him
the situation and asked him for his advice.
He agreed that the girls deserved a taste of
their own medicine, and he said he had a great
idea, but he needed one thing in return.

He then told me he wanted me to go to
the dance with him!!!! I tried not to look as
shocked/horrified as I felt.

All I could manage to say was, "But, what
about Veronica?"

He told me she lost her chance because she was playing games with him and he wasn't going to wait around any more. "So what do you say?" he said.

I was torn. I really wanted Reggie's help, but I also really wanted to go to the dance with Archie! But if I said no to Reggie, I might end up going to the dance ALONE, because who knows if Archie will even ask me at all?

But I guess it's kind of flattering that he asked me... even if I WAS his second choice.

So... I said yes.

And we brainstormed some ideas before we came up with the perfect prank. It's so simple, really!

Remember that photo I took of Veronica wearing the Yeti Thrill wig when she was dancing around?

I decided to show it to the Glossies.

I told them that Veronica's always ahead of the newest fashions and the next big thing is Yeti wigs.

They TOTALLY bought it. They were all like "OMG, So chic!" and "She can pull off ANY style!"

I managed to convince the Glossies that Veronica will be wearing that wig to the dance, so they better show up with wigs of their own if they want to keep up with the trend.

Heh heh heh. I can't WAIT to see them show up in those ridiculous wigs! It'll be worth the wait!

Reggie says the best pranks are the ones that take time to unfold!

I sort of jokingly told him he should write a book on pranks and he said that's his dream project! I can only imagine...

I guess going to the dance with him won't be SO bad... as long as he behaves!

Unfortunately, there's still the dress to deal with! Veronica is bound to notice if I don't end up wearing it, so I decided I had better do something about the stain!

I took it to my local dry cleaner to see if they could help. The lady who works there is always grumpy and makes you feel bad for bringing clothes in. But she always does a good job which is why people keep going back.

Sure enough when I handed the dress over she gave me a guilt trip and was like, "Oh my. This will be hard to get out. You shouldn't be drinking coffee at your age, anyway!"

Blah, blah, blah.

As I was getting ready to leave the dry cleaners, guess who walked in? ARCHIE!!! He totally caught me off guard and I forgot how to use words again.

He said, "Oh, hey, Betty!"

But what came out of my mouth was something like, "Ohio! Yar Arch!"

He told me he was bringing his suit to get dry cleaned before the dance. Then things got REALLY awkward when he said, "So Reggie told me you're going to the dance with him, huh? I didn't think he was your type..."

I told him it was more of a favor, really.

Then Archie said:

Aww, well that's too bad.

THAT'S TOO BAD?! WHAT DOES THAT MEAN?!!! DOES THAT MEAN HE WANTED TO GO TO THE DANCE WITH ME????

Now I'm REALLY wishing I hadn't said yes to Reggie. In fact, I bet if I didn't, my meeting with Archie at the dry cleaners would have gone more like this:

Instead, it was just super AWKWARD and tense. UGH.

He was just like, "Well. I guess I'll see you around, then."

And I tried to come up with something clever or memorable to say in return, but I couldn't think of anything so I just said, "Um. Yeah. I guess. See ya."

The worst thing is knowing that now Archie will probably ask Veronica to the dance, and I'll have to watch them be all romantic! BLARGH!!

Not only that, but guess what? One of the Glossies took a photo on her cell phone when they spilled coffee on my dress. The thing is, the photo was cropped to just show ME, so it looked like it was MY fault the dress got ruined! Then she showed the photo to Veronica. She was LIVID!

Even though I told her I was getting the dress dry cleaned, she was still super mad, and didn't believe me when I told her it was the Glossies who did it! She even went so far as to FIRE me from the planning committee! Can you believe that? She said I'm irresponsible and can't be trusted with important things!

Well, fine! I've decided I don't want to grow up to be a party planner anyway. Not if I have to deal with entitled brats like the Glossies constantly! Man, I can't wait to see them make fools of themselves at the dance! Hehehehe!

And at least I ordered the ice sculptures before Veronica fired me. So my creative vision will be STILL be represented at the dance! Well, that's all for now, Diary. I'll let you know how the dance goes.

Reggie BETTER be on his best behavior!!

♡ Betty Cooper

Homecoming Dance

Dear Diary,

Phew, do I have a lot to write about! Where to begin? As Homecoming got closer and closer, Veronica began to freak out more and more because she STILL didn't have a date. In fact, she couldn't BELIEVE I got a date before she did and she was kind of mad I was going with Reggie since he asked her first.

But it's not my fault she didn't say yes to him when she had the chance! Honestly, I think the REAL reason she's been so cranky is because Archie STILL hasn't asked her to the dance. Secretly, I'm kind of glad, but now I can't help but wonder who he WILL end up asking out. Such a mystery!!

Also, Veronica made me return the green dress after I got it cleaned, so I had to find something else to wear. My mom went dress

shopping with me, but we CLEARLY have different tastes.

My mom made me try on this ridiculous, poofy, frilly dress and was gushing over it saying, "Oh, how ADORABLE! You look like a porcelain doll!"

That's NOT the look I'm going for.

After trying on approximately a billion things, I did end up finding a dress that I liked. It's blue, just like my eyes! But my mom said it made me look like an older woman. Hello? That's perfect! I knew I'd look SO sophisticated! I couldn't wait to wear it out! I even got matching heels (which I still need to practice walking in).

And as much as I hate to admit it, I realized I was actually LOOKING FORWARD to going to the dance with Reggie. Crazy, right? I started seeing him with new eyes. I mean, he IS pretty good looking, and he's got a great sense of humor... even if he can be a bit immature at times...

Since this was going to be my first REAL dance, I realized I'd better actually learn to, well, DANCE! The last thing I wanted to do was make a fool of myself in front of everyone, and step all over Reggie's feet. So I looked up some dance tutorials online and practiced in my room in my spare time.

I have to say, I caught on pretty quick. Maybe a career in dancing is in my future! And then I can do things like make my own dance tutorials (except I would CHARGE for mine, duh), and I could start my own dance crew and we'd clean up the streets with our sick moves. It'd become such big deal that they'd make a movie about us!

Once I had more or less mastered the basic ballroom dance steps from the tutorial, I decided to try it with my heels on, since that's what I'd be wearing at Homecoming.

BAD IDEA!!

First of all, heels and carpet DO NOT MIX. I realize that now.

Whoa!

Secondly, those shoes are hard to dance in, PERIOD. Even when I moved into the driveway to practice, I ended up breaking off one of my heels when it got caught in a crack! I super-glued it back on, but one shoe's now slightly taller than the other. JUST GREAT.

How was I supposed to dance in them NOW?!

I was also starting to get a LITTLE concerned about Reggie. I mean, he asked me to the dance and everything, but he was basically ignoring me at school. Not only that, but as the dance got closer and closer he didn't really tell me what the plan was. Like, was he going to pick me up, or were we just going to meet at the school? Weren't we supposed to get dinner or something before the dance? I had NO idea what was going on!!

I told Veronica about it when she came over one day so we could swap fashion magazines. (We each subscribe to different ones and like to trade them when we're done reading them.)

I figured Veronica would have some good advice since she's more experienced than me when it comes to dating and stuff like that.

I told her I thought it was pretty rude, especially since the dance was tomorrow night and Reggie still hadn't said a word to me about it.

That's when Veronica said, "Um, Betty. I think you need to know something..."

You will NOT believe what Veronica told me. She said that Reggie had practically BEGGED her to go the dance with him and finally she said yes, because Archie STILL hadn't asked her and she didn't want to be dateless. Of course she tried to justify it by saying she wouldn't have said yes if she thought

I was still going to the dance with him. But apparently Reggie didn't even mention my name, so she assumed things were off between me and him!

What.

WHAT!!!

Naturally, I got a LITTLE upset.

That's exactly what I planned to do.

I'm not usually one for confrontation, but I was MAD and needed answers! So when I saw Reggie before class started the next day, I totally asked him why he asked Veronica out if he and I were supposed to be going to the dance together! I didn't even care WHO overheard us--THAT'S how upset I was!

And you know how he responded? By LAUGHING in my face!!

"WHAT is so funny?" I yelled.

Reggie is such a big JERK! He said,
"Remember when I told you that the best
pranks take TIME to unfold?"

That's when I realized that him asking me to
the dance was just his idea of a JOKE!!!

I looked like a complete IDIOT in front of
everyone. I hope Reggie and Veronica enjoy
their stupid dance. They DESERVE each other!

I couldn't wait for school to be over so I could
just go home and faceplant. I can't believe
I was DITCHED on the night of the dance.
I felt like such a loser!!!! I guess the only
consolation is knowing that Veronica isn't going
with Archie after all.

FACEPLANT of DOOM!

My mom and dad came in to ask why I wasn't

getting ready, and I told them that I wasn't going after all. But could they leave it at that? NO. They HAD to ask me WHY, and then they didn't believe my excuses.

Finally I was forced to tell them the truth. My dad was SO mad at Reggie. But then he said something kind of sweet. He said, "Listen, sport, you can't let a jerk like Reggie ruin your night! It's HIS loss and when he sees you in that beautiful dress, he'll be sorry. I'm gonna take you to Homecoming and you're going to have FUN! You don't need a date, especially not one like THAT guy."

It reminded me of when my dad used to coach my little league team and he would give my team the BEST pep-talks whenever we were losing. So I decided to get up and go to bat.

I got dressed for the ball!

My mom even let me borrow her most expensive pair of shoes since my own were still kind of wonky.

I have to admit I looked pretty good. My mom said I looked like a fashion model! My dad said, "Beauty AND brains. I'd call that a home run. Now let's get going, sport!"

Of course, I was feeling all fired up until I actually stepped INTO the dance. Then I felt like a loser all over again and I didn't have my dad there to give me another pep talk.

I looked around to see who Archie ended up coming with, but I didn't see him anywhere. So I decided to go and spend some time admiring the ice sculptures I ordered.

Of course, you can only spend so much time staring at (and talking to) an ice sculpture before you start to look like a crazy person.

Luckily, there was a wonderful distraction!

The Glossies all came in with their dates, wearing those RIDICULOUS wigs! Of course, everyone started laughing at once!

Oh, man! It was SO funny! I was glad I decided to show up after all, just so I could see my prank in action.

When Veronica spotted them, she threw a fit! She started yelling, "Is this your idea of a JOKE? After all the work we put into this dance?"

And the Glossies looked SO confused and were like, "We thought you'd be wearing one too! Honest!"

Veronica was all like, "WHY would I be wearing a wig to the dance?" and then one of the Glossies showed her the photo of her that I took. Oh, man. I don't think I've ever seen Veronica SO MAD.

When Veronica realized it was a photo that I took, she came storming over to me. I swear I saw smoke coming out of her ears.

218

Things got pretty heated and people were starting to gather around us to watch. (NEVER a good sign...)

And then the most amazing thing happened...

Veronica... apologized.

Her actual words were, "You're... you're right, Betty. I didn't think. And... I'm sorry."

Seriously, at first I thought it was another prank, but no! She was being totally sincere!

She said she was so desperate to get a date because no one else asked her out. So she said yes to Reggie without thinking about how it might make me feel, and that it was wrong.

I think I had to pick my jaw up off the floor. I can count on one hand the number of times Veronica has apologized to me in all the years we've been friends.

Well, I then told Veronica I was sorry I leaked that photo of her wearing the yeti wig, and that I was just trying to play a joke on the Glossies. I didn't think it would impact her like it did. I guess we were both kind of guilty of the same thing...

I was glad that Ronnie and I made up, but I still felt kind of awkward being at the dance alone, especially when they started playing slow songs and all the couples started to dance. (Meanwhile, Archie was still nowhere to be seen. Did he decide to skip the dance after all?)

220

WALLFLOWER

I decided to pull a Jughead and hang out by the snack table. At least it looks like you're SOMEWHAT occupied when you're eating chips.

This has been a great snack table so far, huh?

You mean "dance"?

Just then, I noticed Archie walk in... ALONE!

Jughead noticed too. He said, "Looks like Arch' doesn't have a date either."

I told him I was surprised and that I bet any number of girls would have gone with him if he asked.

Then Jughead said the strangest thing...

He said, "Archie's not the type of guy to just go with ANYONE who's available. He'd rather wait for something Betty to come along. I mean, BETTER."

Was that intentional? It certainly got me thinking...

But before I could think about it TOO much, I got distracted by a commotion on the other end of the dance floor. Turns out, Reggie played a prank on Veronica! He sprayed her with Slimy String!

I guess it's a good thing I didn't go to the dance with Reggie after all. Veronica was so upset, she LEFT the dance and dragged the Glossies with her!

This is a DESIGNER dress and that stupid string leaves STAINS! We need to get to a dry cleaner, stat!

But, but, why do WE have to go?

Minutes after Veronica left, they announced the Homecoming King and Queen and invited them to the floor for an official dance. And guess whose names were called? That's right-- Reggie Mantle and Veronica Lodge! AWKWARD.

Reggie may like pranking other people, but he does NOT like to look like a fool himself. Next thing I know, he was trying to convince ME to dance with him instead.

He was like, "Betty, I'm SO sorry I ditched you. Let me make it up to you right now... will you honor me with a dance? You can be my beautiful Homecoming Queen."

And I said, "Sorry, Reggie. You lost your chance. Looks like the joke is on you!"

The look on his face was PRICELESS!

I was feeling pretty empowered so I decided to go and do one more thing before I lost my nerve.

I walked right up to Archie and said, "Will you go to the dance with me?"

And he smiled and said, "I thought you'd never ask!"

He told me he had been meaning to ask me all

along, but he kept chickening out! And then by the time he finally decided to get it over with, he heard I was going with Reggie instead.

I can't believe he was afraid to ask ME! I had no idea I intimidated him that much! Now I kind of wish I had the courage to just ask him sooner... I could have avoided all this drama.

(And... maybe I should have listened to Jughead from the beginning.)

The DJ started playing a romantic song and just like I had always dreamed, Archie took my hand and said, "May I have this dance?"

OMG. I thought I was going to pass out I was so nervous at first. But it ended up being THE most romantic thing EVER!!!! (And I'm SO glad I spent all that time practicing because I didn't step on Archie's feet AT ALL!)

After the dance, we went to Pop's Chocklit Shoppe and shared a sundae. It was SO sweet and old-timey. I felt like we were in one of those black and white movies!

So far, high school is off to a pretty good start. I still may not know what I want to be when I grow up, but I do know I can make any of my dreams a reality as long as I have the courage to just GO FOR IT. I realized I can't just sit around waiting for things to happen, I need to MAKE them happen.

Get it, girl.

THE END

♡ Betty Cooper